"Ryane Nicole Granados is the voice of *The Aves*. She is Zora, who invites us to the Los Angeles neighborhood where she lives with her little sister, Prose, and their mother, Mercy, in the 1980s. Twelve-year-old Zora takes us by the hand and introduces us to all of the characters living and dying in this South LA neighborhood. These vignettes dance in the light of a Southern California dusk, where we look into Prose's penny-colored eyes, dream of love with Roxanne and Tony, dance Sauda's choreography, and walk home from school with Jeanine and Janet. Later, Zora writes for Peacock, and after an evening of window-watching with Prose, she holds her sister's hand tight, and races home to tiptoe around vacuum lines in Mercy's carpet. Zora Neale Hurston is the voice of the American South, but in *The Aves*, Granados is the voice of Zora, a young girl with a voice we all need to hear. Granados navigates these tender years page after beautiful page, so we can dance through Lisa's anger, search for love and identity, dodge tragedy, and gaze toward the sun setting over the 405. In this stunning debut, Granados captures the lives in South LA's blue but smoggy skies." – **Noriko Nakada, author of *Through Eyes Like Mine***

"*The Aves*, by Ryane Nicole Granados, will draw you in like a warm, sparkling wave. The truth of a young Black girl receiving her first pressing comb, the removal of her pigtails, her barrettes casting 'huge shadows on the ground. Shadows that resembled airplanes or birds in flight . . . ' announces her, Zora, spirit. This warm, sparkling wave will bring you to a brilliant coming-of-age story. What will develop of Zora's life journey? Where will these birds take her? This sparkling wave of words is well worth the ride! BRAVA!" – **Alma Luz Villanueva, author of *Song of The Golden Scorpion* and *Gracias***

# THE AVES

RYANE NICOLE GRANADOS

# THE AVES

RYANE NICOLE GRANADOS

*Leapfrog Press*
*New York and London*

The Forest Stewardship Council® is an international non-governmental organisation that promotes environmentally appropriate, socially beneficial, and economically viable management of the world's forests. To learn more visit www.fsc.org

**LEAPFROG GLOBAL FICTION PRIZE WINNER**

## Past Winners of the Leapfrog Global Fiction Prize

2023: *Istanbul Crossing* by Timothy Jay Smith
2023: *The Aves* by Ryane Nicole Granados*
2022: *Rage & Other Cages* by Aimee LaBrie
2022: *Jellyfish Dreaming* by D. K. McCutchen*
2021: *But First You Need a Plan* by K. L. Anderson
2021: *Lost River, 1918* by Faith Shearin*
   *My Sister Lives in the Sea* by Faith Shearin*
2020: *Wife With Knife* by Molly Giles
2019: *Amphibians* by Lara Tupper
2018: *Vanishing: Five Stories* by Cai Emmons
2018: *Why No Goodbye?* by Pamela L. Laskin*
2017: *Trip Wire: Stories* by Sandra Hunter
2016: *The Quality of Mercy* by Katayoun Medhat
2015: *Report from a Burning Place* by George Looney
2015: *The Solace of Monsters* by Laurie Blauner
2014: *The Lonesome Trials of Johnny Riles* by Gregory Hill
2013: *Going Anywhere* by David Armstrong
2012: *Being Dead in South Carolina* by Jacob White
2012: *Lone Wolves* by John Smelcer*
2011: *Dancing at the Gold Monkey* by Allen Learst
2010: *How to Stop Loving Someone* by Joan Connor
2010: *Riding on Duke's Train* by Mick Carlon*
2009: *Billie Girl* by Vickie Weaver

* Young Adult | Middle Grade Fiction
These titles can be bought at: https://bookshop.org/shop/leapfrog

*For My Kids*
*and*
*In Loving Memory of D'Ancee "Say-Say" Barnes*

# THE AVES

Los Angeles, 1980s

As a child, I wore my hair in three pigtails. Mercy parted two in the back and left one on the top of my head, which she brushed to either the left or the right side. She snapped plastic barrettes on the end of each braid and coordinated the colors to match my outfit for that day. With barrettes, I had to be very cautious. I learned this critical rule firsthand. If I flung my head around too fast, or got caught in an unexpected gust of wind, my barrettes assaulted my cheeks, and even worse my eyes, in a flurry of piercing plastic. At recess, if I leaned against the tetherball pole or glided high in the air on the sandbox swings, my barrettes cast huge shadows on the ground – shadows that resembled airplanes or birds in flight, soaring around my head like I was a watchtower or light pole.

Last year, my braided wings flew in for a landing. I no longer wore pigtails and had no use for barrettes. On my 10th birthday, I was initiated into a woman's club that embraced the rituals of leg crossing, nail polishing, and hair pressing. A club I did not want to join but have been told I will remain in for the rest of my life. A club I will supposedly induct my daughter into, and she her daughter, while they too squirm in the salon chair, longing for the days of pigtails instead of pressing combs.

On the morning of the big day, I became overwhelmed with fear. I had heard horror stories about the beauty shop from cousins and neighborhood kids. They told tales of the awful stench of lye relaxers and hair grease sizzling. They warned of the ensnaring fog from the warming stove that hovered over you no matter where you sat. And then there was the dryer that set fire to the back of your neck, making your eyes water from the smoldering air or the plastic cape that Velcroed firmly around your throat, rubbing up and down and up again every time you swallowed. Their warnings rang like church bells, chiming loudly and echoing omens in my ear. And so, on my birthday, in the late afternoon, I climbed up onto two phone books stacked in the revolving chair of the salon and prepared for my fate.

Tear-stained and terrified, I was instructed to hold down my ear with my tiny fingers, such inadequate shields against the scorching teeth of the pressing comb. Smoke from the hot iron fused with Miss Felicia's cigarettes, creating a thick asphyxiating cloud around my face and head. The teardrops, already collected in the corners of my eyes, soon began to roll again down my cheeks. As the smoke filtered through my nose and mouth, I began to cough, which caused my body to thrust forward violently. Miss Felicia yanked my head back into place with a swift jerk of my ponytail. "Look, chile, either sit still or get burned, understand?" I nodded. She rolled her eyes and yanked my ponytail into place again. As the smoke intensified, it spread like a blanket across the diamond-shaped mirror. It continued to rise, but eventually divided when the pale pink ceiling blocked its mounting ascent. Sometimes the smoke would billow above my head like a halo, or a tiara. I wondered what the smoke looked like above Miss Felicia's head, but was too scared to move my neck around and look. With a swift flick of her thumb, she let the ashes of her cigarette fall into an empty Styrofoam cup. At times, she would miss the cup and hit the rim or edge of the mint green counter. The dying ash glistened, sparked, and then disappeared into grayish piles of powder.

Geraldo's voice on TV and the futile clank of the air conditioner mixed vigorously with the booming voices of women, large and loud. Each noise seemed in competition with the other, but eventually the women won, with conversations high-pitched, informal, and profane, all offenses I was continually warned against.

Miss Felicia finished my kitchen and rashly worked her way around to my front edges. The heat from the pressing comb caused beads of sweat to form at my temples. With each stroke, I closed my eyes, held my breath, and counted the seconds before the comb would reach the ends of my hair. One, two, three, four, breathe. One, two, three, four, breathe. Miss Felicia muttered something under her breath, her cigarette cocked firmly in the corner of her mouth. "Damn, chile, you got a lot of hair." This time, she spoke loud enough for me to hear and made direct eye contact in the mirror.

The sun began to set, casting an orange glow throughout the entire shop. It danced between Pete's Liquor, the Wash and Go Laundromat and the Nix check-cashing place. Like hide-and-seek, it played behind a passing truck and then peeked out over the stoplight. The sun revealed the true appearance of the black metal bars that covered the windows and doors. Rusted and chipped from overuse, they were less intimidating than they appeared in the daylight. The approaching night let me know that Mercy would be coming to save me soon. Minutes later, the metal door squeaked. I stretched my eyes as far left as they could go but still could not make out the figure in the doorway. I slightly turned my neck, keeping as much tension as possible in my head. The hot comb barely nipped the corner of my ear, but filled my entire face with a tingling, burning sensation. I flinched and flung my head to the side screaming out, "Mercy!" I lifted my hand to touch my ear, but Miss Felicia slapped it down. She blew hot breath and lumped a swab of grease from a brown jar on and around my burn. After handing me a tissue to wipe my eyes, she said, "I told you not to move."

All my life I've called my mother by her given name of Mercy. When I was younger we lived in my grandparents' house with my uncle, my two aunts, my cousin James, and my grandmother's three birds, Janice, Rocky, and Bird. Everyone including the birds naturally called her Mercy. I suppose I simply picked up on the trend, but somewhere along the line a mother usually checks in and corrects the error of her child's ways. Not Mercy. She decided that "Mother categorizes women into a stereotypical role imposed by society in an attempt to stifle their efforts to break free from the invisible prison bars of home-maker and servant." She told me this when I was seven. Now it's my responsibility to explain this state of affairs to my little sister, Prose, who looks at me with the same blank stare I imagine I gave Mercy. And yet Prose nods, as if she understands, which is simply an additional sign that she has evolved into a full-fledged member of the

Hunter clan. Sometimes we slip up and call her Mom, or maybe Mama, and other times we are relieved to distance ourselves from the Reebok-wearing, dust-detecting, anxiety-stricken nurse who is our mother.

I am confident that Mercy is the only nurse assistant in Southern California who has a fear of diseases, germs, bugs, dirt, household cleaning products, and LA smog. We have been taken to the hospital for ailments ranging from oversleeping and lopsided cheekbones to recurring hangnails and the common cold. She has diagnosed us with diseases we cannot pronounce and healed us with both traditional and herbal remedies learned from her nursing courses at the junior college. She drives us crazy, but she also brings order to our daily lives. A healthy balance between breaking down and growing together is the essence of the Hunter women.

When Mercy reaches her final day, a day she often claims will be premature if Prose and I continue to "test her patience," she has made us promise that we will not wallow in grief, we will not have any regrets, and we will not let the mortuary adorn her in fuchsia or pink lipstick. For some it may be morbid to discuss the funeral arrangements for your perfectly healthy 38-year-old mother, yet for me it's relieving. It's kind of like an instruction manual for memorializing Mercy Hunter.

Mercy leaves instructions for everything. She constantly worries that we won't be prepared for whatever crisis may occur in the event of her absence or untimely death due to an unpronounceable, incurable disease. There are instructions strategically placed around the home for the stove, the washer and dryer, electric outlets, warm water, and hot water, and master lists accompanied by back-up lists with emergency phone numbers for the entire LA County. Once a month we run drills in the event of a fire, earthquake, or a freak Santa Ana windstorm. Prose has been crowned the Queen of Escape because she has broken all the Hunter records for exiting the house in the fastest time. We had a party in her honor because parties are another of Mercy's many traditions.

Mercy says, "Life is a combination of celebrations and unfulfilled expectations." She has committed her mothering years to ensuring we have as much celebration as possible. "Life doles out a healthy dose of disappointment. If you celebrate the little things you'll cope better with the loss of the big." Next week Mercy is throwing a party for me. I came second in her spur-of-the moment natural disaster drill.

I always go last in hopscotch. The order is like this: whoever's name comes first in the alphabet throws first, whoever's name is second goes second, and so on and so on. My first name is Zora, which has secured my place as last in almost every street game we play. When I am not busy waiting for my turn I get the privilege of explaining my name, defending Mercy's odd choice in name picking, and when all else fails resorting to a good old-fashioned "well your mama's so fat she ...." I usually fill in the blank with my newest insult adopted from my cousin James, who stays with us on the weekends while my Aunt Rita goes to school.

My full name is Zora Neale Rebecca Hunter. Zora Neale is after Zora Neale Hurston, Mercy's favorite author, Rebecca is from the Bible – Mercy says everyone needs a good Christian name – and Hunter is the last name of my father, who I rarely get to see, but I have his name as proof that he existed at least before me.

My sister's name is Prose. Prose Leah Hunter. Mercy thought of the name Prose in the hospital after she gave birth. The story goes like this: about 19 hours into labor the doctor realized that the umbilical cord was wrapped around my sister's neck. They operated immediately but when they removed her she was a dull blue color and wasn't moving or crying. They stuck a tube down her throat and sucked out a yellow greenish fluid. My sister began to scream in an ear-splitting pitch that echoed through the halls of Saint Paul's Hospital. She screamed as if testing the volume levels of her newly developed vocal cords. Mercy says the sound of that scream was like the most beautiful short story she had ever heard. She named her Prose, attaching Leah as a middle name because everyone needs a good Christian name, and Hunter, the only thing my sister and I have in common, my father's last romantic gesture with my mom before he moved out of the Aves for good.

I hate my name, from beginning to end. I made the mistake of telling Mercy this once and my error resulted in a two-hour lecture about the significance of having a mother who cared enough to name me honorably. This was followed by a rundown of all the names of the poor children in the neighborhood "whose autograph will have no substance because their parents named them from an empty place. You, Zora, have a name with distinction and privilege. When people say your name they are pronouncing greatness." I didn't dare tell her when people say my name they are pronouncing torture to my ears. When people say my name they say it with a rough Z and an elongated OR, connected to a heightened A. They say my name in a questioning tone as if it were an accident, as if that couldn't be my name. And they look at me. They look through me. They look for an explanation without asking for one. I didn't dare tell her that she is the only one who says my name with distinction. She is the only one who makes it sound meant and right. "Zora" slides off her tongue like melting ice, like savory peach cobbler. "Zora" rolls all together, no rough Z or heightened A, just one quick wisp of a name. Like wind blowing. Like the downstream of a river.

4th Ave

Unlike Mercy, predictably present, party planning, and germophobic, my father is an astronaut, a moonwalker, a star cruiser. Prose and I are the daughters of a rocket-riding explorer. When we were young he left on a top-secret mission. He said, "I'll be back. Girls, don't wait up. I'm off to save the world." Mercy swears he didn't say the last part, but she just didn't hear him. He only said those words to me. When he left I felt a knot the size of a watermelon swell inside my stomach.

While away he misses many memory-makers. Birthdays, funerals, the Prose-goes-to-preschool party, my first dance recital, our move from the apartment on 3rd Ave to the brownstone on 10th and the 2nd Ave School Father-Daughter Dance.

My uncle Ricky escorted me to the dance, which would have been fine if not for the fact that he is only 11 years older than me, thinks the Texas Hop is a fraternity step, and opted for a tuxedo shirt with a bow tie and vest painted on the front instead of spending the money to rent a suit.

My granny taught me how to hit a softball. She did a pretty good job, but at my first game, when the pitcher struck me out, she ran onto the field, cursed and kicked the umpire and then dragged me from the batter's box. It would have been a clean getaway if not for the fact that her bright yellow sun hat with wild orchids sticking out the top became wedged in the doorframe of her Chrysler LeBaron. As we fled the scene she was still turning her head from side to side, tilting the brim of her hat, looking like a wobbly spinning top.

While my father, the astronaut, moonwalker, rocket-riding explorer, is off saving the world, he misses the Prose-goes-to-first-grade party, cousin T.C.'s release from prison, cousin T.C's return to prison, and the emergence of two uninvited guests.

I wake up one day and there they are. No training bra, no warning sign, no trial run, just two imposing mounds. I go from sliding headfirst into home plate to "en pointes" and "high kicks" with backless leotards, from double Dutch at double time to side-sleeping, shoulder-strapping, eye-turning boobs. They are the topic of discussion wherever I go. "What happened?" asks Prose. "Daaaannng!" chime all the boys in the 2<sup>nd</sup> Ave crew. And the one that irritates me the most is Mercy's: "I'm so proud of you." She says this as if I have set out to create these immovable objects.

And now at school my best friends, Jeanine and Janet, are upset because I got 'em first, the boys are cruel and mean because they will never have 'em, and Mrs. Jensen no longer calls on me even when I raise my hand, which I am convinced is due to the fact that mine are bigger than hers.

For weeks after my two new guests move in I go to school, come home, do chores, sleep on my side, and start my day all over again. In class I focus on becoming invisible. I will my existence into the shape of a bird and I think about my plastic barrettes. If only I still had them to help me fly out the window, out the gates of 2nd Ave, out the neighborhood. The brainpower it takes to become a bird in flight clouds my hearing, making it impossible for me to recognize the repetitious, "Miss Hunter. Miss Zora Hunter!" flying from Mrs. Jensen's lips. When I open my eyes everyone is looking at me. Even Jeanine and Janet have set their eyes in my direction.

"Are we interrupting you, Miss Hunter?"

"No, Mrs. Jensen."

"Are you ready to tell us who you will be bringing to Career Day?"

Career Day. The day when children invite their parents to discuss what they do for a living in an attempt to inspire children to work toward a career. Career Day. The day when students pretend to care and parents pretend they actually like what they do to pay the light bill.

"Um, I am going to bring my … father."

"Okay then. It looks like everyone is scheduled."

My father? Even I don't know why I said that. Mercy would never be able to get the time off. She is always working. Someone's always getting sick. My uncle fixes cars with a guy named Titus whose claim to fame is putting five Burger King Whoppers in his mouth at one time. My brain is drained from being a bird. I missed breakfast. My breasts are expanding by the hour. All these things help in the creation of one impossible task: bringing my father to Career Day.

When the Friday of Career Day finally arrives, I know I have to come up with something. I pack the junior scientist mail order telescope James won in the Rice Krispies Box Tops contest and roll up the poster-size map of constellations Mercy brought home from the hospital. I will explain to the class, without divulging too much information, the complicated demands of my father's job.

After Maxine Coleman's dad finishes giving his over-dramatized narrative of life as a plumber, Mrs. Jensen nods in my direction and I come to the front of the class.

I position the telescope on its fold-out legs and hold the map in front of me.

"My father sends his most deepest regrets for not being able to make it to Career Day. He is an astronaut so it would be very difficult for him to make it here from outer space. I thought he might get a special leave but he's working on a top-secret mission." I direct that statement at Mrs. Jensen. "When it is all over I am sure he won't mind coming in and showing everyone his space stuff."

I finish my speech, very proud until the entire class breaks into laughter. Their voices chime like the school tower bell fading and growing interchangeably. The symphony of highs and lows clashes with the whispers of parents quieting their kids. I even think I hear Mrs. Jensen laugh but I can't bear to lower the map I now use to hide my tears in order to look in her direction. I bite down on my lower lip to stop it from quivering and the louder the laughter gets the harder my teeth gnaw into my flesh. It is not until I can taste the salt from my tears mix with the warm blood resting in my mouth that I set my unfortunate lip free. The slap of Mrs. Jensen's ruler on her desk finally interrupts my painful song. She motions me back to my chair and the frown on her face accompanied by my name on the board lets me know that I am in trouble.

When the bell rings, Maxine walks over and says, "My daddy says they ain't lettin' no poor man in space and even if they did no one from around here would be stupid enough to go when we already have enough problems to deal with right here on earth. The only moonwalking your daddy did was out the front door." With that she rolls her eyes and runs to catch up with her father. I attempt to follow her but Mrs. Jensen clears her throat in that *don't you dare move* type of way. I slump down deep into my chair.

"Miss Hunter, I admire your creativity but lying is unacceptable."

"But –"

"No buts. I will have to make a call home to your mother."

I want to say, "Well that's why mine are bigger than yours." I even open my mouth to let the words come out. All that exits is, "Can I go now?"

"You're dismissed."

As I walk out of the room I think I hear her laugh again. I begin to run furiously down the hall. I run out of the school, through the schoolyard gate, up the alley, and around Pete's Liquor Store. On 4th Ave I meet up with Jeanine and Janet. To let me know they are no longer mad at me, they begin to run too. We take all the shortcuts our parents forbid us to take. We cut through Mrs. Jackson's backyard and hop the fence behind the abandoned crack house. We sprint across the parking lot of First Zion Baptist Church and dart across Main Street with its broken traffic signal, dodging oncoming cars, leaving the crossing guard chasing behind us. We race between the townhomes on 8th Ave and across the community garden on 9th. Janet stops to pick a flower and meets up with Jeanine and me catching our breath on my back steps. By this time the warm air has dried my tears only to make way for fresh new ones. Jeanine and Janet reach under their tops and hand me their tissue boobs they have been wearing for the last two weeks.

James is standing on the footstool in the kitchen laughing hysterically through the back window. "Ain't no use crying now. Your mom got the call and is on her way home from work. I'm s'pose to tell you not to go anywhere. An astronaut, a freakin' astronaut. I always knew you were a space case."

The sky turns purple and then black before Mercy makes it home. I spend the time in between watching the headlights of passing cars hit my wall and then slide onto my ceiling. I wait for the one that would shine directly into my window to let me know the Honda Accord has pulled in the driveway. When the waiting gets boring I close my eyes as tight as I can and then open them slowly, allowing the colored circles that appear when you do that type of thing to bounce off of each other and melt back into blackness. Eventually I just listen to the ticking of the mahogany clock that hangs on the wall in the hallway mixed with the soft taps on the door from Prose dutifully checking on me. The ticks and taps lull me to sleep. It is not until Mercy flips on the light switch, startling me awake, that I realize she has made it home.

I drop my pants and begin crying before I even feel the sharp wind of the belt moving mid-swing. I flinch twice before I realize I'm not getting hit.

"Lying is wrong. I've raised you to be an honest person. You mustn't lie. Even when the truth hurts so much that the lie becomes the only way to lessen the pain, you still mustn't lie."

She yanks up my pants and turns me around to face her. A pool of tears sits in the basin of her eyes. She rubs the sides of her forehead as if trying to massage away her thoughts. We remain in silence interrupted only by the theme to *Star Wars* being hummed by James as he walks down the hall.

"The worst kind of lie is the lie you tell yourself. When you lie to yourself you cheat yourself out of the opportunity to grow from the pain you feel. There are three types of hurt: the hurt you use to hurt others, the hurt you use to hurt yourself and the hurt you use to be of use. Don't accept uselessness just because he did."

It is one year, nine months, and 17 days before we see our father again. He missed the Prose-goes-to-the-dentist party, James's graduation from middle school, and the emergence of Jeanine and Janet's four long-awaited guests.

He stays for a week this time. He has a room at the Ramada near school and each day he strolls by the chain wire fence hoping to catch a glimpse of my pigtails, not realizing I no longer wear them. He tries going by the house to see Prose but she doesn't want to see him and dives under the dining room table to hide from the man she has only seen in pictures. On the last day, he greets me with a teddy bear and two giant-size pixie sticks. I loved pixie sticks when I was nine, but now I'm 12. The gifts let me know that he is leaving again. It hurts less this time. Only a small knot the size of an acorn rests in my stomach.

The taxi pulls up and waits impatiently. He kisses me on the forehead, twice. One for me and one for Prose. He has gained weight since the last time and his poked-out belly presses painfully against my chest. The taxicab driver gets out and opens the passenger door, an obvious indication that he is ready to go. As they drive off the bumper sticker on the cab reads, *Hollywood, The Place for the Stars*.

5th Ave

After the astronaut affair of the 2nd Ave School Career Day, Mercy feels it might be good for me to talk to our church pastor. Only murderers, adulterers, or grieving mothers of kids killed too soon must speak to the pastor. I'm not sure if Mercy is worried that my sinful lying might lead to a deviant life of crime, but I overhear her on the phone telling Deacon Hayes that she needs the pastor to get a message across to me. She says she can't continue to do this by herself. For the first time Mercy sounds breakable. I tell myself I won't mess up anymore, or at least anymore this year.

James keeps telling Prose I'm trying to give Mercy an ulcer, which is caused by stress and can lead to internal implosion, sort of like a soda can shaken and then opened. He learned something like this in biology and has chosen to add his own twist including hands-on examples such as the six-pack of Orange Crush he and Prose waste emulating Mercy's eminent death.

When we approach Solid Rock Christian Fellowship the church bell chimes. It rings three times. One for the Father, one for the Son, and one for the Holy Ghost. Mercy's stride is quick and Prose's is quicker. I race to catch up with them, adjusting my oversized stockings every three or four strides. I hurry past the usher handing me an offering envelope and the order of services only to find that Mercy and Prose have already entered the church. Mercy looks back at me only once and yet the look carries a lifetime of reprimands. This is the type of look that causes both eyebrows to curve inward into a capital M and both eyes to squint as if too pained to widen to their regular size. This look is always accompanied by a stiff neck and tightly pressed lips. This look, whether Mercy admits it, is a traditional mother look that says, "Get over here …," "Don't make me call your name one more time …," "When we get home …," and the infamous "I can't believe I went through countless hours of labor for this." This look conducts an entire conversation without words, and this look is disappearing into the assembly of morning worshippers all hurrying to give praise.

I rush through the crowd bunched at the door. By this time, the choir has begun their usual drone to the tune of "What a Friend We Have in Jesus." An elderly woman in a bright green bonnet sways and hums in agreement. Her hands are stretched upward to the sky. My "Excuse me, ma'am," is drowned out in her "Hallelujah!" I step one way and she sways in front of me. Step. Sway. Step. Sway. If I don't reach her church pew soon Mercy is going to kill me in the house of the Lord. I take a deep breath, stutter step, and dodge around the hat.

Inside the church a potpourri of smells greets me. Cologne, perfume, and the potent pine of aged and over-used wooden pews mixes with the saturated smell of used leather Bibles passed down for generations. A familiar hand taps my elbow and I slide into the seat next to Prose. She whispers, "I win." I nod. Mercy looks over to show me the M-shaped-eyebrow eye squint of disapproval. I sigh.

The pastor approaches the pulpit.

"Today, Church, we're going to talk about the Big 'H.' Not Heaven or Hell, not the Holy Spirit, but the big 'H' of honesty."

Mercy looks again in my direction.

The congregation cries, "Amen," in unison.

"Honesty," repeats the pastor. "Being honest with yourself, being honest with those around you, and most importantly being honest with God."

"Amen!"

"Are you truly honest or are you simply honest when it's convenient? Do you make excuses for your lies? Are you honest in your giving of God's 10 percent in the collection plate? Are you honest about your commitment to God? None of us are free from sin, but today, Church, we're going to free ourselves from the bondage of our lies."

"Yes Lord," says a woman in the first pew.

"Preach," says a voice from behind.

"Hallelujah!" screams the woman in the green bonnet.

The sermon sounds like Pastor Baldwin is speaking directly to me. Could Mercy have actually convinced him to devote an entire service to my sinful ways? I look over at her and she gives me another standard mother look. This one is the exact opposite of the other. Both eyes widen and the head cocks slightly to the left or the right depending on what angle the look is being shot at. This look has a very simple translation. It means I'm looking in the wrong direction and paying attention to the wrong thing. In this case it means, *Turn back toward Pastor Baldwin immediately.*

The pastor continues his discourse on honesty and sin and lies and salvation and all things right and wrong in this world. His words seem to run together while his lips hurry to catch up with them. My mind begins to wander, yet I know I need to pay attention. Along with Mercy's desire to throw parties goes her compulsion to administer pop quizzes. I will undoubtedly be asked to paraphrase Pastor Baldwin's sermon against the untruth as proof that I have been delivered from my wicked ways.

While my mind struggles to commit scriptures to memory and interject amens in accordance with the congregation, my body is tangled in its own personal struggle of sweat against nylon and Lycra. My pantyhose are stuck to the edge of my pew and they tighten around my waist as I try to break free from the seat that imprisons

26

me. I do all of this while attempting to keep my upper body completely still so as to not nudge Prose, whose head is nestled comfortably between Mercy's arm and her sheepskin purse.

A cotton candy sky forces its way through the stained glass windows and beams streaks of color across the entire church. Its light reflects tiny rainbows in the beads of sweat that rest above Prose's lip and around the nape of her neck. I admire the rainbow. I envy it. How something so beautiful can both expand and shrink to touch things big and small amazes me. If I were to throw a party, I'd throw it for the rainbow.

A gruff old man nudging me with the collection plate interrupts my thoughts. The usher I'd rushed past in the lobby smugly hands me an offering envelope.

"Honesty," urges the pastor.

"Amen," cries the church.

"Amen," I say under my breath, yet I am one second too late.

I feel Mercy looking at me and silently instructing me to look back. I turn my eyes in her direction to see her wink back in mine. Another mother look, this one meaning that I am forgiven.

Mercy's best friend died today. Today, Tuesday, at 4:11 p.m., she died. Her husband called the house but Mercy wasn't home. The waiting is the hardest part. What do you do while you're waiting to tell your mother that her best friend in the whole world is dead? I can't cry even though I feel I am supposed to. Her husband cried so loud he sounded like a symphony of sorrow. His cries echo in my head and yet my eyes seem powerless to produce water.

Her name was Sauda, which means "dark complexion" in Swahili. Sauda's name was the only name on our street that made sense. She was the brownest Black person in our entire neighborhood. I'm the brownest person in my family and everyone says I get that from my father's side that I never get to see, but Sauda was the brownest person I've ever seen. And she was pretty. When she smiled her skin lit up like she had light bulbs in her cheeks, and ebony rings circled half-moons around her eyes. She looked as if she'd been dipped in ink, and she was curvy with clothes that tied her up like brass ribbons.

Mercy says Sauda was born in Africa but moved to California when she was just a little girl. Her father was a doctor back in Kenya but when they came here, he could only get a job as a janitor and then a factory worker. Sauda's only daughter, Imani, is two years older than me and she once claimed that she was a direct descendant from royalty because she had true African blood in her. She said my blood was mixed with white people's blood because my hair was too fine and slippery to come from pure Black ancestry. I told her to shut up because I'm the brownest Black person in my family due to my father's side that I never get to see and if I wasn't Black, how come my hair crinkled up like a curly fry when I forgot my umbrella in the rain, and how come when I wash it, it shrinks like the time Mercy put my We Are The World T-shirt in the dryer on high? And so it was settled: we were both African Princesses. We pricked our fingers and mixed royal blood-lines to make our nobility official.

Many evenings Sauda would invite us into her den to drape our heads and shoulders in bright kente and elegant silk. We listened to jumbled fragments of African folktales told by Sauda's father who came to live with them when he got the disease that makes you forget things, sometimes even who you are. We could only play dress-up Mondays through Wednesdays because on Thursdays all the moms on the block got together to talk and on Fridays, whatever plans they cooked up on Thursdays were put into action. As time passed we just stopped playing the game altogether. We never really looked the part. We never looked as royal as Sauda.

Sauda was more than pretty. She was enchanting. She would choreograph elaborate dance routines and all the girls in the neighborhood practiced in her garage until we got every count and every turn synchronized. Even Lisa next door, who couldn't dance at all, was never left out of the routine. Sauda said that dancing was a device of the heart and not the body. So Lisa, rhythmically hopeless, was designated by Sauda as our dancing muse. Before every performance Lisa ran around us in circles flailing her arms and rotating her hips as if balancing an imaginary Hula-Hoop on her tiny waist and buckling knees. On the fourth Saturday of each month we performed for the old ladies who sat on porches coughing, cursing, and swapping neighborhood gossip mixed with Bible verses, cigarette smoke and gin. When we finished they would clap and high-five each other, talking in a virtual scream about "back in the days" when their hips would spin out of control. Sauda always said we did a good thing for them; we took them back to a place they could only reach in their minds. We smiled as if that was our sole intention. Sauda laughed because she knew we really just wanted to dance. The boys in the neighborhood dreamed of dribbling a basketball to fame. Us girls would pirouette our way to a better life.

Sometimes during the summer, when the nights seemed hotter than the days and we slept in tanks and underwear with windows open and thin sheets for covers, Sauda would sit on her porch strumming the strings of her guitar and singing poetry into the damp night. Her voice was hypnotic, drawing us out of our homes and onto her front lawn. Young girls with babies of their own would rock them to sleep to the tune of Sauda's sonnet. On these nights Mercy would dig out her old poems. She kept them in a box in the top of her closet that said *don't touch* without ever being written on. On these nights Sauda would sing Mercy's poetry and Mercy would become free. No bills, no collection agents, no cleaning, no scoldings, no homework to check, no lectures to give, just Sauda, Sauda's Spanish guitar, Mercy's don't-touch box, and freedom. On these nights Sauda's husband fell in love with her all over again. On these nights he didn't drink after work, and he no longer wore the look of a man whose dreams had disappointed him. On these nights he looked at Sauda as if she was the beauty we all saw each day. His eyes squinted as if trying to awake from a dream and his lips curved into a grin so unfamiliar to his face.

Today Mercy's best friend died. It's 5:30 and Mercy won't be home for at least another hour. I'm waiting to tell her and I suppose I should be crying. Prose cried for over an hour and is now sitting under the dining room table with her face swollen like a puffer fish. Imani is away for the summer visiting her cousins in Arkansas. I wonder who will tell her. I think about Imani and I want to cry for her. Sauda died of the cancer, but we won't find that out until later. She just couldn't breathe in life anymore. She gave up. I wonder if Mercy will be angry. Mercy hates quitters.

I want to turn on the television but Sauda died today. I shouldn't want to watch TV. I figure leaving the TV off, at least for Sauda, is the respectful thing to do. Instead I stare out the window. Two boys are kicking rocks up the street while punching each other simultaneously. Sauda's husband is sitting on the front porch hugging her Spanish guitar. Lisa is on the sidewalk practicing her arm movements. I feel like I should tell her we won't be dancing anymore, but I don't. Marcus, the neighbor from up the street, comes careening around the corner blowing his horn and swerving back and forth. He's holding something out of his window. As he approaches I can tell it's a cigar. He's screaming but I can't make out the words. I open the window and swing my legs over the sill, waving in his direction. He speeds as if headed directly for the house and screams, "It's a girl, Zora! It's a baby girl!" Marcus's girlfriend had a baby girl today. Tears finally roll down my cheeks.

**7th Ave**

Mercy's mourning for Sauda is done in private. We hear her cry in the bathroom, but once she comes out each day, she is dressed in her hospital scrubs and her face is as dry as a desert. There is little evidence of her tears, except her voice, which sounds like she is underwater gurgling out her instructions for the day. We know better than to say much of anything in return. The flood is right there inside of her and when I manage to get kicked out of Sunday school, I am pretty certain Mercy's dam is going to break.

I want to read the part of God in the church play but Ms. Davis, the Sunday school teacher, says I can't because I am a girl. Mercy always tells us girls can do anything that boys can do. I share this with Ms. Davis and she asks if I am challenging the fact that God is a man. It isn't until after I reply that I realize this question is one of those questions adults ask, but you're not really supposed to give them an answer back.

"I think God is a man and a woman. He's like a pocket mirror that you open up and look into. If you're good and didn't lie or anything that day, when you look into the mirror you will see the face of God. That's why people say God is inside of us. God is us on our good day."

The girls in the class made up of Jeanine, Janet, myself, and some girl who is here visiting her grandmother from Tupelo, Mississippi, all begin to cheer.

"Silence, children! Silence!"

Ms. Davis shakes her finger at me so angrily I think her Lee Press On Nails might fall off.

"Are you actually sitting in the house of the Lord calling God a pocket mirror?"

This time her sharp tone cuts like a knife, leaving no doubt that this is one of those unanswerable questions.

"Miss Hunter, you leave this class immediately. Wait outside the main sanctuary for your mother and you pray. Ask our merciful God to forgive your sacrilegious soul."

While I pray the only thing I can think to say is, "God, please don't let the church play suck. Elijah can barely read and Travis, the only other boy in our Sunday school class old enough to play the part, laughs uncontrollably when he gets nervous. Amen. Oh yeah, and forgive me for my sacrilegious soul. Amen again."

The only thing Mercy says when she and Prose get to the church is, "I bet Sauda would love to see you read the

36

part of God." Then Mercy looks up at the roof-mounted cross as if she can see Sauda's smile and laughs so hard she cries.

When my sister, Prose, was born, I wanted her to be a boy. Selfishly I worried that if she was the same gender as me I would have to share my stuff with her. I often set out to show her that I was boss. Yet no matter what I did, from hiding her bassinet behind the couch because she wouldn't stop crying for a bottle to convincing her that cleaning our room was a requirement to earn a permanent position in the family, her face was never without love for me. Eventually I realize her face is never without love for most people, but with me, she always manages to have my back or be right by my side.

I am not sure if Mercy's half-laughing, half-crying church episode is an official get-out-of-jail-free card, but Prose bringing home a homeless man a few days later is certain to bail me out of trouble. The worst I ever did was bring home a guinea pig from school and Mercy sent him back the next morning, criticizing me for giving her yet another living thing to feed. But Prose, she really does it this time. She brings home a real living breathing man covered in windblown dust and grime, holding a cardboard sign that reads, *If you think your life is hard, try living mine.*

I've actually seen the man before. He stands on the corner up the street from our favorite pizza place, ToGo, sometimes asking for money, but usually he's just sitting under the shade of the covered bus bench, his bench that no one else dares sit on.

When I explain to Prose his situation, her response is simple and Prose-like. "If he doesn't have a home, then he needs a home." Sometimes when we pass him, I let her give him our school lunch leftovers. An apple slice or Fruit Roll-Up and my sandwich when it's peanut butter day, my least favorite. He thanks us in a scratchy voice that squeaks like a rusted, unused bike chain.

One day Prose gives the man a card that she made in her afternoon art class. It has stars colored in Ultra Blue, Prose's favorite Crayola color, and it has a picture of a house on it with a guy standing on the porch. I tell her don't give it to him because it will make him sad that he doesn't have a home to live in, but she insists, telling me that this card is going to make everything all better. I don't argue with her any further.

A week later, as we're walking around the corner onto our street, I see a man in the distance standing on our porch. Prose breaks into a full-speed sprint screaming frantically, "He came, he really came!"

The card that Prose gave the homeless man wasn't really a card at all. It was an invitation with our address on it. The man hands me the note to read after seeing the awkward look on my face. Now my voice is the one that is prickly and hard to use.

"Sir, I'm sorry but we're not having anything here. My sister is just …"

"Actually, Miss, you don't have to explain. I didn't come for any sort of party. I was figuring the young girl was simply trying to be sweet and I was over this way so I wanted to drop something off to her."

Prose grins from ear to ear as if this man is actually going to present her with an extravagant gift. Instead he hands her his trademark sign and on the back it reads a simply stated *Thank You*. Prose hugs him and cheers as if he has given her a million dollars.

"I've never had a cardboard sign before. It's so big, but not too heavy. Thanks."

Me and the man with no home exchange grins while Prose runs circles around us holding her new sign high up in the sky.

9th Ave

Imani came home today.

After Sauda's funeral, she returned to Arkansas to live with her aunt and cousins. It's been three months since she left 10th Ave and four months since Sauda died. Word around the neighborhood was that Imani's father would likely never visit her because it would be too painful to see his deceased wife's image melt into the face of his maturing daughter. So we all said our goodbyes and I figured it would be the last time we'd see Imani. People born on the Aves rarely leave the Aves and even fewer find themselves on a plane headed back. Imani, however, had a different plan. She saved all the money she earned waitressing at A Taste of Africa, her cousin's restaurant, and she took a Greyhound back to Los Angeles, back to 10th Ave.

Lisa sees Imani first and proceeds to make the rounds. In a matter of 11 minutes, everyone in the neighborhood knows that Imani has returned. Lisa boasts that it would have been under eight but the ice cream truck broke down again and she hit a roadblock made up of grade-schoolers swarming the circus-themed truck.

I bribe Prose with two dollars and a Chick-O-Stick to get her to stay at home while I go to see Imani. Prose has this thing about asking questions. A lot of questions. I do not want Imani's welcome home to become one of Prose's full-scale examinations. Although she only lives two houses away it takes me over an hour to reach her front door. The first 55 minutes is spent thinking of what I would say and the next 25 minutes is spent convincing Prose that I'm not leaving her home alone and instead am merely leaving her 130 feet away from me.

Before I knock on the screen, Imani opens the door.

"Oh, dang, were you leaving?"

"No. I heard steps. I hoped it was my father. Have you seen him?"

"Sorry. No. I haven't seen him for at least two days."

There is a long silence attached to a clear look of disappointment that veils over Imani's face. I stand with one foot on the porch and one foot on the frame of the door with Imani's two feet planted firmly in front of my right K-Swiss, an indication that I am not being invited in.

"Is this a bad time? I just wanted to welcome you back. None of us really got to talk to you before you left, and you know how it is on the Aves, we all figured we'd never see you again and –"

"Come in, Zora. I was just really hoping that it was my father."

There is something in the way Imani speaks. Something older and steadier. She doesn't sound like a 14-year-old girl and she makes me feel much younger than 12. When I enter the house, I see her clearly, unlike at first when the metal frame of the screen door cast a phantom-like shadow over one side of her face. In the living room she stands before me looking like the living dead. Something in the tilt of her head and the arch in her back resembles her mother's dead body brought back to life.

"So are you here visiting or something?"

"No, I'm back. This is my home. This is where my family is."

"Yeah, I hear you. Your dad is going to be real happy to see you. Mercy has been to the home a couple of times to check on your grandpa too."

"Yeah, she wrote my aunt and told her. How does my father look?"

"The same, I guess. I mean, he goes to the sanitation department, comes home, and then leaves back out."

"He's going to the bar, Zora. At the bus station I ran into Jimmy's dad from 6th who used to work the door at the First Down and he said that Raymond's brother over on 3rd told him that Elvin the bartender is upset because my father left yesterday without closing his tab."

"Well Elvin's always mad so one more thing's not going to make much difference. I'm sure if your dad pays him back today, it'll be fine."

"Yeah, but that's not all. His bed doesn't look slept in, so I'm thinking he didn't come home at all last night."

"I'm sure he'll be home real soon. That's one thing about your dad. He always works hard and he always comes home – eventually."

Imani does not respond to my attempts at comfort, yet her silence assures me that she knows there is some truth to my words. As we sit drenched in our thoughts I notice that the house looks exactly the same as it did on the day of the funeral. There is even a stack of napkins that Mercy gave me to hand out at the repast sitting exactly where I left them four months earlier. Unused and stacked on the edge of the cherry wood dinette table, they sit in wait as if any minute now they will be put to use. All of the shades are drawn, shedding only slivers of light through the corners of the window where the curtains fail to meet the sill. The pause button on the tape deck is still pressed down. I imagine if I press it again the house will fill with the throaty inflections of The Whispers or maybe even Earth Wind and Fire. Imani's dad clearly has not touched a thing since the day his wife's body was covered by the earth.

"I know everything sucks right now, but I'm glad you're home, Mani."

Imani leans her bare calf into my extended leg.

"I'm glad I'm back too."

"I'm gonna let you unpack and stuff and Mercy is work-ing a double shift so I'm kind of stuck with Prose all day but you can come by if you feel like it. The Aves haven't been the same since …."

Silence feels better than saying, *since Sauda died.*

When I walk outside the daylight is a harsh blow. In a downward squint I see a steel-toed work boot coming into view. Looking up, my eyes meet with the heavy-hearted gaze of Imani's father. He touches me on my shoulder as he passes. When I reach my front steps, I look back and notice Imani has opened the door for him.

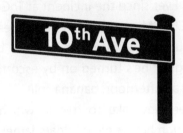

One thing that's great about little sisters is the fact that they're only as smart as you allow them to be. Although I gave Prose two dollars to stay put while I went to talk to Imani, later that afternoon I resourcefully convince her to treat her big sister to a slice of pizza and a medium RC Cola. She has pepperoni, I have greasy cheese, and together we share a scoop of rainbow sherbet.

We meet up with Jeanine and Janet at ToGo around 2:00. The hour between 2:00 and 3:00 is key at ToGo because that's the time when Jim, the manager, does the books. This is also important because Jim's mother comes in to cover the register and she's always cold so Jim has to turn the freezer down where the ice cream is displayed. This is most consequential because ToGo has the cheapest ice cream in the Aves and yet the coldest ice cream in all of South Los Angeles. One scoop is grounds for a record-breaking brain freeze. This one kid, who used to go to 2<sup>nd</sup> Ave Elementary but now gets bused to the gifted kids' school, chipped his front tooth on a spoonful of cookies and cream. I don't even remember his real name. Ever since the incident at ToGo, everyone just calls him Chip. My cousin James also uses ToGo in his constant pursuit to hook up with girls. He brags about all the "headlights" he's turned on by escorting clueless classmates for an afternoon banana split.

"The longer they take to decide which flavor the brighter their high beams glow," gloats James.

ToGo is not the real name of our favorite pizza spot. It's Jim's Pizza even though the sign no longer says so. The hand-painted signpost that hangs above the swivel door is scratched and faded from years of summer scorchers and random rainy days. The brownish red *JIM'S PI* has become a safe haven for pigeons looking for a place to rest their wings, find some shade, and relieve themselves on unsuspecting passersby. When entering ToGo I always remind Prose it's like a dance. Stay light on our feet, go in one at a time, and be cautious yet quick. A rushed group impatiently entering all at once will find that their heads are a perfect bullseye for pasty pigeon poop.

We have been calling it ToGo for as long as I can remember and you can tell when someone is in town visiting the Aves because they complicate matters looking for menus and signs and directions when there are only two options: pizza (cheese or pepperoni) and ice cream, for here or to go. The name ToGo developed out of Jim's unchanging catch phrase used to greet customers entering *JIM'S PI*.

"Forhere or ToGo?" saluted Jim.

He would say "for here," so quickly and overlaid with such a strong Korean accent, that "ToGo" for many years was all that anyone could make out. That accompanied by the fact that there is only one table, clearly made for two yet adjoined by three hardwood chairs with wobbly legs and jagged corners, prompts most to respond with an emphatic "To go, Jim." This exchange has become somewhat of a ritual at ToGo. Jim asks a question that he surely must know the answer to and everyone responds as if this is the first time that they have been propositioned in such a manner. Only visitors who come from some unfamiliar land would choose "for here."

There's only two places to eat once we get our pizza and ice cream. There is the curb adjacent to the Laundromat, but we have to quickly get up when cars approach to park, many of which barely stop until they have taken out the curb, our pizza, and almost us with their car bumper. Then there is the bench in front of the beauty supply, but every time someone walks in or out the blast of wind that immediately follows is notorious for taking our entire pizza plate with it. This week we choose the bench. I am still not confident that Prose has successfully mastered the grab, jump back, slide over technique needed to survive our curbside meal, but because she is Prose, she is hopeful about it. She is what Mercy refers to as a true optimist.

Prose, with her eyes the color of pennies, sees the richness in even the most unpleasant of situations. Prose sees things the way they should be, and when those things don't come to be she feels sad but never sad enough to stop expecting. I envy Prose's expectancy. I don't expect much and maybe that's why much never happens. Something is bound to happen for Prose. She's looking for it while the rest of us don't even know where to look. When Prose sleeps, her eyelids flutter as if still looking in her dreams – Prose and her copper-colored eyes on a treasure hunt even in her sleep.

Sometimes Prose and I go for window walks. Our walks are perfectly timed following a trip to ToGo because that's when Mercy starts her dust-free derby. She doesn't ask for help. She says we never get it just right, but she does decide there is to be no walking on the mopped floors, no stepping on the strategic vacuum lines painting the carpet's canvas, no sitting on the fanatically fluffed couch, and most importantly no breathing near the streak-free windows, mirrors, glassware, and Clorox-cleansed countertops. And so we walk, around the block and around the block again because the suits haven't come to build a stoplight at the corner. To cross the street at dark would be to indulge in a game of hit and miss, cars against pedestrians.

Before Sauda died she started a petition where everyone on the Aves signed their name. She declared, "The suits will have to listen because the written letter is timeless and confirms that we were here and we cared and we fought back." During this speech Mercy nodded in agreement and followed with, "The biggest revolutions are fought on paper. Let's revolt." But we still walk around the block because scribbled signatures weren't as effective as we hoped they would be. So still no suits, still no crosswalk, just Mercy's cleaning. Prose and I walking.

As we walk, the sun settles behind the 405 and the streetlamps buzz until they can finally find the strength to burst open with light. Then, as if an electrically charged current runs beneath the roadway of the Aves, porch lights, kitchen lights, and living room televisions, headlights bound for home and city lights leaping across the sky shine brilliantly throughout the streets. Prose has decided that the evening tide is God's daily Fourth of July.

You can see so much more when you walk the streets than the portrait revealed from a passenger-seat window. You can see the goings-on of families sitting down to dinner, friends swapping saucy secrets, marriages breaking up, husbands returning home, babies' first steps, boys' first kisses, girls' first taste of the reality that their fathers are not invincible and their mothers don't have all the answers. When window-walking, the soul of the world rests between the drawn curtains of Los Angeles.

Miss Maige lives in the window, three sprinkler heads away. On the first floor, behind the oak wood door, within the pale-yellow walls sprouting up from the forest-green carpet seen through the four-foot glass pane, is Miss

Maige quilting the kinfolk of kinfolk into a lineage of linen. A family quilt to be passed down from Ave to Ave as the covering for visiting grandchildren, the drape protecting the house from the quick-witted wind outsmarting the loose brick designed to plug the apartment hole. A family quilt that tells the story of stories for all who climb under and listen.

Roxanne lives in the window above Ms. Maige, only 17 but on her own because the suits say there's no longer room for her in the foster home. And so the suits lower her rent and send her checks every month and the suits come by to make sure she goes to school and has no one else living there. Roxanne will be 18 in a few months and will have to find a business suit of her own.

Roxanne has a lover who she kisses at night. He's 19 and he's enlisted in the Marine Corps. When he visits, he scares off the stoop squatters who wait for her to walk home from school. They don't whistle anymore, but they still watch. They watch the straps of her backpack trace the sides of her breasts and they long to be the weighty books that bounce off the back of her acid wash jeans.

While Roxanne's lover fights to defend her magnificence, she enjoys the hungry eyes that reside in the stoop squatters' stares. She rolls her hips and bites her bottom lip, giving them the thrill of a lifetime, as if a supermodel on her own personal runway. When she reaches her steps she makes sure to look back. She makes sure that they're positioned and then she blows their minds. Softly, as if kissing satin, Roxanne presses the palm of her hand against her full lips and gives wings to a flirtatious kiss. Her admirers lean over the railing of the stoop as if catching a foul ball hit into the stands at Dodger Stadium. They cheer and slap high fives and then quickly turn to make sure Roxanne's lover isn't patrolling the Aves.

He knows nothing of her daily ritual. When he comes calling, he finds her waiting in the window. Waiting and reading. The books once housed in her bouncing bag now lie sprawled out on the living room floor. For Roxanne these books hold the secrets to life. Roxanne reads and waits for her lover's return. She reads out loud to herself so that the breath of each story can dance a waltz in her ears. She reads until she hears the starched stiffness of his solider uniform scaling the stairs.

"Hey, bookworm, tell me a story," he says. And she does. Roxanne retells the accounts of Tish and Fonny on Beale Street and Romeo and Juliet in Italy. From beginning to end, he listens and then rewards her with a kiss. He kisses her in the dimly lit corners of the room and of her body. Their shadows melt together, creating a silhouette of tenderness for all who walk by to see.

Sometimes when Prose and I window-walk, Roxanne peeks over her shoulder similar to the way she glances at the stoop squatters and she winks at us. She winks while we watch until her lover's hand fumbles for the curtain's edge, sliding it closed and capturing their love inside.

56

In the window across from kissing Roxanne live Marcus, Ketura, and their six-month-old daughter, Baby-girl. When she was born they had yet to decide on a name, but when Mercy stopped by to pass down the crib that James had slept in, and I had slept in, and Prose had played in because she liked the way the night sky colored the spaces between the crib bars more than she enjoyed sleeping, Mercy gave Babygirl the name of a queen. Born on the day of Sauda's passing, Babygirl's given name is Danielle Sauda Hall. Sauda because it's only fitting for a baby that looks doused in dark chocolate, Sauda because it creates a legacy of strength and power to be reborn in the future of the Aves, Sauda because "It was simply the right thing to do," explained Mercy. And Danielle after Daniel because everyone needs a good Christian name. Like Zora, Sauda is the type of name a baby has to grow into. Until then, for her sake, I'll call her Babygirl.

In the window below Babygirl's crib you'll find the Viramontes women untangling their tresses. Angela, pronounced Anhella, Viramontes is in my grade and has been in my P.E. class for the past three years. Every day, no matter what the occasion, she wears her hair in one long braid that she winds and winds and winds again until a neat bun rises above the nape of her neck like a freshly baked donut almost too perfect to eat. I hate the bun she wears to camouflage the curls. Our window-walk-ing exposes a wave of thick black hair long enough to sit on and strong enough to swing from. If I owned her windstorm of hair I would spin in circles, letting its length cloak me like a superhero's cape. I would frustrate my enemies by flinging my hair on their desk as they tried to complete their vocabulary words during journal writing time. I would run my hand from scalp to hair's end and roll each strand around my index finger to get the attention of the cute older boys. I would brush it 100 strokes a day to keep its shine like the fashion magazines suggest. I would wash it with strawberry shampoo and let the suds sink in until the entire bathroom smelled like the strawberry patches of Orange County. I would do so much if I had Angela's, pronounced Anhella's, hair, but I would never, no matter what my sisters did, or mother did, or brothers expected, or father demanded, wrap it away from the eyes of the world.

Every apartment has four windows that face the sidewalks paved up and down the Aves. Each window is a camera lens revealing a picture of the Aves' soul. When Prose and I window-walk we're photographers taking mental photos and Prose often cups her hand into circles around her eyes as if she's a top-secret agent peeking through binoculars at unsuspecting targets.

When the sun reaches the base of the 405, only the moonlight guides our path between the spread-too-far-apart streetlights with flickering bulbs struggling to stay alive. And when the cars have found their way home or the porch lights have sighted the last key in the lock, it means it is time to end our window-walking tour. We can smell the aroma of the Aves. Orange and blue gas flames on Sears layaway Kenmore stoves work hard at stretching enough for two into a meal for five. The stoves' heat and the frying pans' grease create a screen of suffocation between the half kitchen, dining room, living room areas. Windows fly open, freeing the smoke and smells and culinary creations to give sustenance to the starving belly of the Aves.

Prose grabs my hand because she's old enough to exist as an undercover agent and curious enough to watch Roxanne's lover cup her entire breast like a baseball glove, yet she's scared of the night sounds and shadowy images that accompany our return home. The humming in the streetlamps seems louder, the arguments in the apartments are clearer, and the figures from the bus stop or the next block are threatening until they get close enough to reveal their familiar face. I would never admit this to Prose, but I need to hold her hand too.

When we get home, Mercy is waiting on the porch. After every housecleaning and every window walking, she waits and replies with the same lists of remarks. With our fingers behind our back we count down her catalog of criticism. One, "Where have you been?" Two, "You better have not tried to cross that street at night." Three, "You know it makes me uncomfortable when you stay out this late." Four, "You're not little boys, you know, you're girls." Five, "You do know this, right?" Six, "I don't know where I got you two from." Seven, "Dinner's ready, hurry inside."

And as we run up the stairs we stop at the door's edge to allow Mercy her one final statement. Eight, "Girrrrlllllsss, take those scruffy shoes off and don't mess up the lines on the carpet." We giggle, but never loud enough for her to hear as we tiptoe acrobatically around the carpet's edge.

Roxanne is getting married today.

Her lover, Tony, proposed four months ago on her 18th birthday. A week later she said yes. I overheard her explaining to the church mothers that it was not because she didn't love him but rather because he was all that she had ever loved. Her game of pop fly kisses with the guys on the Aves never went further than the last porch step. And Roxanne also professed that the rumors of her affairs tearing foster families apart were just lies made up by insecure wives and their husbands who had wandering eyes. And so it was only Tony who had ever entered her sacredness. It was only Tony who knew the taste of her collarbone or the smell of her rising love. Even the mother board suggested she might take a few other cars for a ride before buying the Buick and then they shushed themselves realizing that I was still in the room waiting for Mercy to pick up Prose's wings for the Angel of the Lord part in the Christmas play. I am certain they resumed their chatter once they saw Mercy and I and the angel wings awkwardly parade through the wooden church doors.

I don't know the final word that transformed *maybe* into *yes*, but today, the day before Communion Sunday, the Aves is having a wedding and all are invited.

Solid Rock Christian Fellowship sits at the beginning and the end of 1<sup>st</sup> Avenue. It is only fitting that the altar where Ave residents are christened at birth and the altar where Ave causalities are eulogized at death is both the entrance and the exit to the imaginary gates of the Avenue homes. Because the neighborhood is designed in the shape of a horseshoe you must drive through and around leaving the same way that you came in. It is for this reason that many elders say it's nearly impossible to make it out of the Aves. "No one wants to go back through what they just barely got through in order to come out on the other side." But Mercy says we "shouldn't listen to old bitter tongues," and, "If we knew what was good for us we'd just move in the opposite direction heading out as hope lost people head in."

Those who accidentally wander inside, those who don't live here and are only down this way because they were told this is where the best fried fish can be found, those who speed through in the hopes that their shiny television-like cars won't attract too much attention as they buy highs and sell dreams don't see what I see in this U-shaped block. On any given day you'll find history revealing itself as the future change creators excel on asphalt and chalkboards despite the unlucky horseshoe that they call home. Those who accidentally wander inside don't see the exquisite treasure or swelling potential erupting through brick and bars and concrete backyards; there's very little grass and yet there are seeds and harvest and produce and weddings at the altar where those who accidentally wander in speed by.

Roxanne is wearing white lace and Tony is wearing his military uniform that makes him look much older than 20. Prose spent all morning picking the flowers that now lie strewn on the church floor. Mercy, Imani, Ketura, and I are bridesmaids, which gives me a front-row view of the exchange of I do's. Tony's eyes are watery and he blinks often as if trying to make sure the woman across from him is still really there. Roxanne's eyes remain fixated on the white rose in his lapel. White roses are her favorite. Everyone on the Aves knows that Tony is allergic to roses yet he makes his weekly ritual to the community garden to create a bouquet that is carried by his hands and the force of his sneezes all the way to Roxanne's front door. I suspect these are the things that transform *maybe* into *yes*. When Roxanne's turn comes she says, "I do," loudly. Loud enough to smother any doubt. Loud enough to bend the edges of the white rose away from the bud's center.

The pastor soon introduces them as husband and wife and Roxanne and Tony exchange a most disappointing kiss. Their lips barely part and Tony's hands stay rigidly at his side like a soldier standing at attention. The slow dance of tongues now looks like strangers meeting for the very first time. Prose even looks cheated as she tries to poke her head between Ketura and Mercy's hips. The organist plays the song that little girls practice their wedding walk to and Roxanne escorts her husband back down the aisle.

I too think about getting married one day, but the only boy who talks to me regularly is my cousin James. If he weren't my cousin I'd probably have a crush on him too, as it seems every girl on the Aves is jonesing for some quality time with James. My crush on James would be different though. Not a sickening *I want to marry my actual cousin and have his kids or pretend it's his lips that I am kissing when Jeanine, Janet, and I practice our technique on the backs of our hands* type of crush. My crush would be different, a deeper crush. A crush that makes me want to be where he is, to have what he has because James is the ultimate definition of cool.

Everyone wants to be around James. At 15 he's invited to all the quinces, school dances, and backyard barbecues. Girls hold their breath and check their hair when James enters a room. Guys poke their chests out and invite him to stand around and watch the girls that hold their breath and check their hair. Teachers are amazed at how James can appear to not be listening yet always have the right answer whenever called on. Coaches say he could go pro, football and basketball, at a big school that plays big games that even get shown on TV.

I feel proud and noticed around James because he's fly and everyone knows he's fly. The guy I marry one day will be fly too. But I won't hold my breath and check my hair when my fly guy walks into a room because I'll be fly too. Together we'll be fly and when he kisses me I'll feel it everywhere, even on the backs of my hands.

14th Ave

The Aves are filled with mostly boys. I once remember hearing the ladies at the beauty shop talking about how there are always more men than women, something about competition and conspiracy and why women can't catch a break. I've actually never really counted the girls versus the boys but in the Aves you know there are more boys because they are louder wherever they go.

Their high fives and hollers sound like the base speakers pumping out of my uncle's hatchback and they don't talk, they scream. From one end of the block to the other or even if they are standing side by side it's always, "Yoooooooooo Derrick, Suuuuuuup James, Heeyyyyyyy Q." They stretch their syllables like thick caramel and Laffy Taffy. Their voices take up all the air as they stroll.

The girls on the Aves are more whispers, but that's because we always have secrets to share. It's the classified information exchanged between us that validates our bond. Crushes and wishes and games of MASH reveal our hopes for the future and our friendships are built solid by bricks of secrecy. Brick by brick by brick. Sometimes the weight of the secrets feels heavy but it's the lifting weights that makes us strong.

Lisa has been getting stronger too. Ever since Sauda died all she does is practice her dancing. A lot of us haven't found the heart to dance, but Lisa's front lawn is her stage. Last week, I got a glimpse of the Lisa show, beat by beat. The incessant fighting of her parents was drowned out by the blaring of Paula Abdul's "The Way That You Love Me." Lisa danced in triple time, combining all the moves ever taught to her by Sauda. She did high kicks and held up an imaginary skirt as if she were a French woman doing the cancan. She clapped her hands and slapped her legs like the Blacks of the South dancing the juba. Her acrobatic feats displayed a jazzy jitterbug and a sexy bossa nova. She foxtrotted in a complex combination, then she cha-cha'd until the beat dropped, which was followed by a moonwalk down the block. My favorite part was when she added in all the dance moves that we loved but Sauda thought were silly: the cabbage patch, the running man, the robo cop, and the wop. Lisa's moves were lively, violent, deliberate, and sharp. She danced. Paula sang, and then she stopped. Lisa ejected the cassette tape and walked back into the house as if exiting stage left at the end of a Broadway performance.

I wanted to scream, "Encore! Encore! Again! Again!"

And for a moment it appeared that she had read my pleading thoughts because she burst back through the screen door like a star forced to acknowledge the clamors of her adoring fans, but to my disappointment she angrily grabbed the boom box like a child who had misbehaved and she stormed back into the house, ending the recital for good.

On cue her parents' concert, a mêlée of shouts with breaking glass, was taken off mute to resume loudly in steady discord. I thought I was the only who saw Lisa's performance, but as I rose to give her my standing O, I saw the Peacock staring at me as I stared at Lisa.

She looms like the sun baking the asphalt, watching candy-coated kids skateboarding, bike riding, and triple-dog-daring in a game of spin the bottle. She comes when the school bell ceases to ring and the chalkboards fade from green to ashy gray. She's a sign of summer, only appearing when spring has said its farewell. In her eyes, LA actually does have seasons. The season to disappear into her triple-bolted, chain-linked hideaway and the season to wear the sun's singe and her rose-colored glasses.

Every day during summer break, we walk by her on the way to Pete's Liquor Store. She sits watchfully on a crate in the corner of her porch and, in between swift looks from right to left as if any minute now someone will be coming, she writes on her stationery. After each sheet she pulls out a bottle of perfume from her flower-printed housecoat and sprays the page, fans it a little, presses it up against her slight nose and then neatly folds it in half, only to stuff it in her other coat pocket.

We used to do cruel things to her. Jeanine, Janet, and I stood lookout while James and his friends hid in the brush beneath her porch lying in wait. When she was settled, having strategically placed her crate so that she had a clear view from one end of the block to the other, they would blow into the fire siren noisemaker James made from his Scout's Society survival pack and she would bolt.

Like a peacock with fluorescent feathers, her flowered housecoat blew as she raced back up the stairs into her dungeon of captivity. We clowned about the Peacock the entire day and many days that followed, until Prose, who "liked the flower lady and her pretty glasses," told Mercy of our antics. For an entire summer Mercy made us trim the hedges around building 108 while our Peacock with the red eyes sat in silence. We were instructed to cut them slim enough so that there was a clear view around the steps, creating an impossible fort for the brainchild of cruelty. We were also pelted by flying rocks targeted at our new defendant and thrown by kids without conscience-driven siblings. For an entire month we protected our precious Peacock, until her assailants got bored and moved on to another victim. Our job now done, the Peacock could write on.

Today on the way to Pete's we are stopped by the yellow ribbons of police crime tape that drape off the corner and restrain angry residents from tearing into the streets. Jeanine, Janet, and Prose want to go look. I decline, no longer attracted to the chalk lines of picked-off pedestrians. Instead of hardening, my stomach gets weaker at the continued sight of blood. My knees feel wobblier and I even start to have bad dreams. Familiar faces made out of blood-splattered asphalt, concrete pavers, and shards of glass interrupt my sleep.

"You guys go ahead. I'm gonna chill here."

"You scared?" sneers Janet.

"Naw, I'm just over it."

"Can I go, Zora?" Prose asks.

"Sure, whatever. Hold their hands."

Together the three amigos strut off and I head the other way. At the same time a plane flies over the Aves, headed in the direction of LAX. It seems low enough and loud enough that I wonder if the passengers can see me. I bet I look like a tiny brown creature slinking away from yellow slime.

"Not your speed, huh?"

Wrapped up in my thoughts, I walk three steps away from the uneven voice before I realize it is the Peacock who has spoken. Unsteadily, I take three steps back.

Again I hear, "Not your speed, huh?"

Swinging my right leg slowly in front of my left, I twist to face her but my voice won't speak.

Without even looking up from her stationery she continues our one-sided conversation.

"Yeah, I'm not into it either. I'm more of a high-profile celebrity divorce fan if I might say so myself."

I can't tell if she is joking. I can hardly tell whether she is talking to me or to the letters she attentively scribbles on the page.

Words do gymnastics in my mind. I blurt out the first thing that sounds like English.

"I didn't know you could talk."

As soon as they cartwheel out of my mouth, I want to take the words back.

"I should be offended, but I'm not. Until today I wasn't sure if you had a mind of your own. You surprised me. Today I watched you walk in the opposite direction of the crowd. There may be hope for you yet."

"Huh?"

"Then again, maybe not."

I want a long, fancy sentence to throw back at her. I don't mean to insult her, but it is clear that she definitely wants to insult me.

This time, a pathetic back spring of "Can I go now, Miss?" is all that flies out.

"You can do whatever you want. That is what I am trying to get you to see. Do you have some place to be?"

In that one question she feeds me the stomach-aching reality of my life. I never have any place to be. I sit down on the porch steps.

The minutes tick away as I watch two smoggy clouds merge into one giant blob of gray. The silence seems like one more of her insults. If I am going to sit here, the least she can do is talk to me.

"So you have a lot of people to send letters to?"

"Who said I'm writing letters?"

"Well, you're writing on stationery."

"Is that what they teach you in school? Stationery is for writing letters?"

I am stumped, but not for long. She isn't going to push my mute button yet.

"No, I learned that on my own. They don't teach us anything in school."

"Well that is one of the smartest statements you've made yet. In answer to your underlying question, I am writing what I see."

"Will you read what you see to me?"

<u>On the Bottom Step</u>
*Peeking eyes. Bangs too long to witness the world's wonders. Tiny body. Obese spirit. Hasn't a clue of her story. Overwhelmed by the upsurge of her glory.*

"If you're writing about me, please stop it."

"You are what I see."

Under my breath I mutter something that would have me pruning this woman's flowers for the next five summers if Mercy were to ever find out.

"I'm sorry. I couldn't hear what you said."

She is challenging me.

"I said … I am surprised that you can see anything behind your silly glasses."

For the first time I look directly at her. Up close I realize the glasses aren't really rose colored at all. They are closer to a pale pink, like decorated lips faded from a kiss. They also aren't that silly looking, which means once again she has won in the battle of words. They fit her slender face like a personally customized mask poised perfectly on the bridge of her arched nose.

That evening I am haunted with curiosity and confusion. "Hasn't a clue of her story. Overwhelmed by the upsurge of her glory." In many ways the Peacock is right. I don't know my story, but then again, who does? There is no family dry cleaner waiting for my inheritance like the old reruns of the movin' on up Jeffersons. What little that existed in my college fund set up by late Uncle Freddie was used as a deposit on building 117, now known as the Hunters' Haven. Glory for me is spitting the farthest in a loogie race against James and the boys. I admit I don't know my story, and beyond the psychic woman who reads the cards by night and runs a tax refund business by day, I doubt anyone can claim to truly know theirs either.

The following morning I turn down a day of hanging out underneath the school's oversized oak tree, a common plotting ground for bored kids assessing the plan for any afternoon games. Instead, I pace strategically up the Aves and back again hoping that the Peacock might show her colors. I am about to give up when I hear the familiar sound of a voice not talking to me but talking about me:

<u>Zora's Zephyr</u>
*She walks with a wisdom waiting to wave hello*
*She talks with an intention destined to generate growth*
*She observes with an owl's eye the wonders of her globe*
*She is Zora like her namesake*
*Leaving Dust Tracks on A Road*

"Hey," is all that I can respond, and I am surprised she doesn't reply with "hay is for horses" the way Mercy usually does when I greet people with such casual conversation openers. I refuse to press my luck by asking what a Zephyr is. Instead I need answers. I am there to learn about my story and the supposed surfacing of my glory. It is clear from our talk yesterday that I can't come straight out and ask a question. With that approach I am sure to get an even trickier question as my answer. Instead I come armed with a plea.

"I'd love to know about your story."

There is a long, intimidating silence that makes me wonder if she heard my request. I part my lips and prepare to repeat myself when the Peacock responds, "You don't really want to know my story; it is yours you are hoping to hear." The truth rephrased in her comment carries a disappointed tone, leaving me feeling guilty for my selfishness. I promise myself that, once I hear my story, I will ask her again about hers.

"Zora, do you know who you are named after?"

"Yes, Zora Neale Hurston. A writer that Mercy, um, I mean my mother, likes."

"I hope that is not the answer she gave you when she told you the story of your name. You are called in the name of the teller of tales. Much more than a writer. More like a word slinger. Zora Neale Hurston told the stories of the people in their rawest, rooted existence. Her words are thrown out into the world like a boomerang and they always return home. There's a survival spirit in her writing. People bent but not broken.

Twisting and turning. Boomeranging through strong winds."

The Peacock is perceptive enough to recognize that much of what she says hangs in the thought net of my mind. She pauses as if thinking of an easier way to express her excitement and then starts again.

"You know how you want to do something that you know is right and you know is good and you know maybe one day others will be touched by your courage, but every time you try to do it or you think about doing it or you talk about doing it someone says, 'Get those thoughts out of your head.' Imagine if you did what you wanted to do anyway. No matter what anyone thought, imagine if you did Zora's will. That is what your namesake did. In her writings she wrote her vision of the world. A world where art and individuality have a two-story home."

At this moment I recall Lisa and her dancing display. I want to dance too. Not just for the women on the stoop who Sauda held in high esteem. Not just in the living room in front of the TV and Don and his *Soul Train* entourage. I want to dance like they dance on a real Hollywood stage. I want to bow dramatically while adoring fans cheer my name. I want to dance for Mercy and Prose and Sauda and James and I want to dance for me.

As promised, after learning of my story, I ask in my most sincere tone,

"What is your story?"

She sighs, closes her eyes, and flings her head back in that reflective way that adults do when they are trying to decide if you can handle the real version of the facts or just the PG-rated description of what happened. After a lengthy stillness with her head upturned to the sky, she begins.

"Everything starts and ends with love. Love of another, love of yourself, love of a dream, love of love. In the end, it will be love that saves your life and it will be love that takes it. I have loved many things, but there are two that serve as the bookends for my life story. By love, I don't mean that 'obligatory, because you have to, because it is the right thing to do' type of love that one has for a parent or a child or a sibling or a lame dog. I mean that heart-wrenching, nauseating, maddening, reckless, liberating, life-changing kind of love. The love that tears you apart yet keeps you coming back for more. The tsunami type that takes over and takes you with it. The love that makes you and not the love you make, because you can have it with your clothes on, with just your eyes or even a smile."

She barely slows down for me to get a word in. Like a last turn at double Dutch where you don't want to waste it hitting the ropes, I watch, I time, I watch, I perch, I close my eyes and jump in.

"You make it sound like this love is both good and bad."

"This love is neither; it just is. The problem occurs when you have these two loves at the same time. The good and the bad are when these loves come in competition with

80

the other, forcing your hand, demanding that you make a choice. He was Nelson Shepard and she was my music."

My eyes grow larger with each detail she gives. I feel my lashes touching the tops of my lids, captivated by the discovery that I am finally going to hear from a real adult about love. No more being hushed into corners and other rooms because it is "grown folk" business.

"I loved Nelson from the first time I heard him play. He was a saxophone player down at the Music Note on 5th Ave, what is now the Mann Theater. On Tuesday nights, writers, artists, musicians, and activists would get together and share their passions over bad gin and good company. At the Music Note both women and men smoked and cursed and sang and complained. He stood out because all he did was play. He was impartial to politics, dulled by alcohol, aggravated by smoke, and indifferent to the women who flitted around him with hand-me-down high heels and cheap perfume. He played and he left. Always out the back door and never through the front."

While she speaks, her writing hand relentlessly rubs her right knee, like a genie rubbing a lamp for that final and most wanted wish. In her left hand, her pen lays awkwardly, resting on her middle finger and teeter-tottering from the weight of her pointer finger and the lifelessness of her thumb.

There are gaps in her story. From what I can piece together the Peacock and this Mister Nelson both worked at the same club. In between long pauses she intersperses:

"Are you following me?"

I am trying.

She doesn't wait for a confirmation before she begins again.

"After each performance, he barreled through the Music Note's heavy metal door at 11:10, tugged on his hat at 11:11, breathed in the night air at 11:12, and walked. Not just any walk but the walk of a man with an impatient destination. Rumor had it, he lived only three blocks up, no roommate, no woman, no pet, and no lease longer than six months. He passed by so quickly I actually had to jog to catch up with him. My heavy breathing mixed with the shuffling of my overstuffed handbag got his attention before I ever said hello.

"'Is something wrong?' he asked with an apathy that bordered on insulting.

"I said, 'Yes, something is wrong. No matter how much I stare at you, how hard I smile, how enthusiastically I clap, even on your half-hearted nights, you have never said anything to me. And furthermore, you always leave before I ever get a chance to sing my song.'

"'Well for the record, Isabelle,' he said, 'I have heard you sing. You sang at Martin's gallery opening in his basement last year. You were pretty good.'

"I was too shocked by the fact that he knew my name to be offended by his mediocre response to my singing."

While the Peacock rehashes her shock, I sort out a surprise of my own. The woman in the colored glasses, the poet, the Peacock, is Isabelle. The name is impressive and it fits her well.

She goes on. "I asked him, 'Where are you headed off to so soon?'

"He said, 'I'm headed home.'

"Again no emotion. But his cold shoulder, which was originally facing forward as if in mid-sentence he might just walk away, had swiveled around to face me.

"He said, 'Maybe the better question is who are you headed home to?'"

At this point I am amazed at the exactness with which she retells her romantic encounter. At no time do I question the accuracy of her statements. She recaps each quote like a newscaster watching the whole thing happen all over again.

"'I'm headed home to my four-year-old son.'

"And there it was: the music man had a child.

"'Where is his mother?'

"'At Memorial Park Cemetery.' Again, no emotion.

"What started out as a flirtatious game had somehow turned into a depressing love song," she says.

"'I'm sorry, I'll let you go.'

"Grinning, he replied, 'Where are you headed off to so soon?'

"With just the slightest raise of his upper lip, contorting the deep-set cleft in his chin, my infatuation instantaneously transformed into love.

"For months it was me, Nelson, and Nelson Jr., affectionately called 'Little One.' I was flattered when Nelson admitted that he never really brought women home to meet his son. I was pleased when he felt confident enough to leave Nelson alone with me on nights when I wasn't singing and he was booked to perform. I was moved when he began to write smooth jazz tunes, dissimilar to his usually complex compositions. He expressed that his new songs were inspired by the harmonious relationship the three of us shared. I was irritated when his evening sets turned into weekend gigs, which grew into weeklong trips leaving me with Little One. I was floored when he fired the babysitter without talking with me, resulting in my new title becoming substitute mommy first and songwriter second. I was resentful for the walls closing in as I stubbed my toe on toy blocks that filled what was now *our* one-bedroom apartment. I was in love and in hate all in the same instant. Looking back I probably could have handled the situation better, but on one of his longer trips I re-hired the babysitter, exchanged a tearful goodbye with a sleeping Little One, and I left. This actually was not meant to be a final goodbye. I imagined he would realize he was taking me for granted and ask to start things over again. After six months passed and mutual friends kept reporting to me the whereabouts of his local sets, performances I wasn't invited to, I realized we had spun our last chorus. When you ask me about my story, you're asking about everyone's story including yours. The story of life is a love story. My love for Nelson was complicated by my love for my music. Nelson's love for me was complicated by his love for his son. And in the end we found ourselves right back at the beginning of the song realizing the record had been skipping all along."

"So do you sit here writing songs of regret?"

"Regret is a wasted emotion, Zora. Envision a life that when you grow old you will one day want to remember it, and then spend the time in between making that life come true."

Imani is missing.

She was supposed to begin ninth grade this year and although I'm starting the eighth we decided we would still walk to school together, parting ways at the corner, her going left to Benjamin High and me going right to Madison Middle.

On the first day of school I don't see her. I am even late to Mrs. Barnes's class because I waited and waited, leaning my whole body out into the street looking for her long legs and plaid pleated skirt to wrap around 10th Ave and onto 9th. Because Imani is so much taller than me, I always see her legs well before I see her face; it's as if they are a separate part of her body moving intently, urging her to follow. Three days, then four, then five, then two whole weeks. No Imani. No legs. Imani is missing and no one seems to notice but me.

When I mention Imani's absence to the girls, we plot an elaborate plan to find her. Lack of money, an inherent distrust of the police, and being scared away by the Doberman pinscher in Imani's backyard all result in still no Imani. It is Prose who suggests we just knock on the door but she doesn't realize that life is never that simple … or maybe it is.

If anyone would know how to find someone it's Lou. Lou is the neighborhood salesman. Whatever people on the Aves need, from a new stove to new shoes to even a 30-millimeter camera with one of those professional tripods that real photographers use, Lou can get it. Lou's an older man but it's hard to tell exactly what his age is. His skin is tight, not saggy like the old men who sit in the park playing chess or checkers, their cigars tilted in their mouths and taken out for sudden coughs and deep raspy chatter.

We always know when Lou is coming down the street. He's always in one of his four suits and endless pairs of shiny leather shoes, and the jingling change in his pocket announces his arrival. He accepts all kinds of payment, including food stamps and even pennies. It is rumored that he once accepted 5,000 pennies for a color TV.

Lou lives on the corner of 6<sup>th</sup> Ave and he makes his daily rounds with pit stops at the barbershop, gas station, Bible study, and corner bar. Ave by Ave, he checks in with faithful clients, some happy to see him, others with long overdue IOUs hanging over their heads quickly avoiding him.

I asked Mercy once where Lou gets all of his stuff and she simply responded, "It's America. The land of the free." She said this as if Lou was an American symbol.

My teacher says Lou is a dangerous lawbreaker, a thief, a criminal and we should be mindful to keep away from him.

On this day there is no keeping away from Lou. Down on my knees, frustrated by my failing efforts to outline our hopscotch lines with the edge of a penny while Prose explores the curbside for a rock or broken bottle, Lou makes his midweek arrival. This time in a bright red suit with matching red leather shoes, he comes gliding around the corner with a trash bag thrown over his shoulder. As he gets closer we can hear the clink-clink of change bouncing around in his pockets mixed with the sound of freshly starched pants rubbing together with each step. The bag bounces on his back causing him to grunt at times, and when he passes by us he hands me an electronic Pac Man game and Prose a "Barbie-like" dress-up doll. Without even turning his head he screams back, "Make sure you tell your mother there is more where that came from!"

"I will, sir, but can you do me a favor and keep an eye out for Imani? If you see her can you tell her I'm looking for her?"

"Sure thing, Hun. Sure thing."

"Zora. Psst. Zora. Do you think Mr. Lou is him?"

"What, Prose? Who?"

"Santa Claus. Do you think he's Santa Claus?" Prose whispers her revelation with a toothy grin, feeling accomplished as if she has discovered confidential information.

Back on my knees, I explain, "Prose, there is no Santa Claus."

She demands, "Zora, he is our Santa. Not like the round, white one on TV but a Santa just for us, a Santa for the Aves."

"Okay, why not, Prose? But let's keep it our secret. Don't tell anyone in the neighborhood that you think Lou is Santa."

"You think so too now, right, Zora?"

"Right."

I figure every kid deserves a Santa. While I know the truth, Prose's truth is sweeter. That afternoon Lou gives each child in the neighborhood a toy. Mercy takes ours and demands that we never accept anything from him again. Prose, convinced that Lou is her long-awaited Saint Nick, politely explains to Mercy, "He will be coming back around Christmas and he told us to tell you there is more –" I nudge Prose, which is our sign for *shut up*. She winks, closing both eyes because she hasn't figured out how to close just one, indicating that she remembers Santa Lou is our little secret.

Not too many kids in the neighborhood have the hearts to believe in Santa. With countless Christmases marked by hand-me-down clothes and toys to share, we all eventually discover that Santa and his reindeer have no intention of landing on the rooftops of the Aves. Prose, always determined to prove me wrong, has found us a Santa today. A Santa named Lou, with two legs as his sleigh and his very own jingling bells. A Santa that to me seems more like Christ. Not all of him, but his hands. Hands that have probably touched every other hand on the Aves. Hands that are the only part of his body that look his age, rough and fat knuckled, with wrinkles like road maps tracking the comings and goings of an entire neighborhood. Lou's hands, hands like Jesus. In his palms are the sinners and saints of the world.

19th Ave

Four whole weeks and still no Imani. I tell Mercy and she tries to convince me that Imani probably takes a different way to school now that she is in high school. I explain that our way is the only way and besides, we had agreed to walk together. This prompts a lecture from Mercy about choices and options and being open to new opportunities.

My phone calls to Imani have gone unreturned, my knocks on the door unanswered. I try to catch her father one day as he comes home from work and he pretends he doesn't hear me call his name, yet I see him peek over his shoulder as he fumbles with the lock as if being chased by a juvenile delinquent. Imani's disappearance is becoming a mystery that has to be solved. Mercy insists that she spoke to Imani's dad and all was well, yet five weeks, six and seven – still no legs. It is up to me now.

Monday morning I complain to Mercy about stomach pains too unbearable to deal with at school. I resort to the only benefit I have seen thus far from the bleeding that crept up in the heat of the summer, in my favorite Jordache jeans, thankfully unnoticed by James and Aaron and Q who had unhappily agreed to let me into their game of kickball when their fourth player didn't show. With only half an hour until I need to be sitting in class pretending to be interested in a lecture on the 13 colonies, I decide to take advantage of my unfortunate condition by telling Mercy that I have cramps. She goes on to explain that I must learn to cope with my womanhood. Accept it as a part of my life. As a last-ditch effort, I force tears to well up in my eyes by staring into the hallway light bulb. Surprisingly, she gives in.

After Mercy leaves for work, I wait about an hour and then head over to Imani's. I take Prose's advice and simply knock on the door. I stuff some beef jerky in my pocket in case I need to toss the killer beast out back a treat.

The house is like a fortress. It reminds me of the forts that James, Prose, and I used to make in the living room, only with pillows and couch cushions as our castle walls. Imani's fortress is made up of bolted doors and windows stuck shut from years of paint and repaint. It would take the strength of five men to open the window from the outside. I move to the doors, knocking on the front and back to no response. I move back to the windows, peeking in every pane only to see the dusty backs of unopened mini blinds. I knock on the door again, but this time to the tune of our favorite jam, JJ Fad's "Supersonic." I bang out, "The 'S' is for 'super' and the 'U' is for 'unique.'" After a long pause, I hear the base beat knocking of "The 'P' is for 'perfection'" followed by the click of one lock, then the other, and Imani's whisper of my name.

The living room is dark and it is hard to see Imani's face from where she stands in the kitchen archway. I open the blinds just slightly enough to shed light into the living area. The stripes of sun reveal a ghostly image. I blink twice, unsure of whether I am seeing the living dead or my 15-year-old friend.

"Zora."

She whispers, so I whisper even though I am sure there is no one else in the house who could hear us. "Imani?"

"Zora." Again she barely speaks my name as if it is all she has left in her to do.

I look at her closely. The Imani that I see whose legs never made it to the halls of high school is the reincarnation of her deceased mother. Her hair has been cut into a short bob just below her ears, and although it is a kitchen job it is just convincing enough to resemble Sauda. She wears Sauda's housecoat and Sauda's oversized sweats. But most frightening of all is the wedding band, her mother's ring, worn on Imani's left ring finger, with tape on the bottom to make it fit.

"It's because he misses her so much. Because we miss her."

"But –"

"But nothing."

This time she speaks loudly, in a tone much older than 15. "I'm a woman now. You're still a kid with lots more to learn. I understand my womanhood."

That word "womanhood" echoes in my ear. Mercy spoke of it as the acceptance of pain and Imani seems to believe the same way.

"In a few years I'll be 18 and by then he'll be gone anyway. According to his doctor his drinking has poisoned his liver. It's killing him, my father will die just like my mother, and I – well, I will start again."

All this talk of death is making me cold. The windows are still sealed shut but shivers move up my neck and behind my ear, tickling my skin and causing me to itch uncontrollably.

"You can't tell anyone, Z. Not anyone. Besides, there is nothing to tell except that my father will soon die and be back with my mother, which is the only place he knows to be."

Imani, standing three inches taller than me, stands with her chin to my forehead and squeezes my shoulders.

"If anyone finds out, I will know you told."

She squeezes tighter. It hurts.

"If you want to do anything for me, check me out some books from the library. Anything, something they're reading in high school. I still plan to graduate, you know."

"Imani" is all that I have left in me to say. I turn back toward the window and close the blinds. "Imani. Imani." Maybe if I say her name enough she will remember who she is. When I turn around she has already made her way into the kitchen. She is washing dishes and humming one of Sauda's songs as I let myself out.

There was another accident on 8th Ave today. 8th is an awkward sort of street that looks like it was meant to be a dead end and yet the street maker changed his mind at the last minute and decided to turn right. If not the street maker then maybe nature forced the dirt and the cement and now the houses on 8th Ave to curve like candy canes at the top bend where 8th Ave turns. After the loop the street gets smaller with barely enough room for one car and no sidewalk for pedestrians to walk. Whatever or whoever caused this unusual street shape will now never admit it or accept the blame. Not after the number of lives that have been stolen by cars zooming around with no stop sign urging them to brake and no streetlight demanding that they stop. Whoever or whatever is at fault for this has much grief and many graves resting on their soul.

In today's accident, it looks like the man will live, or at least that's what Mr. Gardner, my P.E. teacher, says. The man is pretty tall and was struck right below the knees, so according to Mr. G no vital organs were likely damaged. The driver wasn't hurt physically, but the image of a man's face colliding with the window shield, splat like bird droppings on the glass and then the hood and then eventually the steamy blacktop, left the woman behind the wheel as unhinged as the kneecaps of the man she had smashed into.

Family members and friends of 8<sup>th</sup> Ave victims have created an altar to honor the dead. Fresh flowers and dying ones alongside candles with religious saints and pictures and fliers and favorite stuffed animals sit on the corner almost in the exact spot where a crosswalk should be. Sauda, Mercy, and even Mr. Lou used to have meetings with suits who would make promises that if enough signatures were signed and enough votes collected a shiny red stop sign could be our grand prize. Broken promises led to more broken bones, more broken hearts, and eventually a rotating schedule of Ave residents trying to add a third part-time job to their daily duties, this one as an unpaid crossing guard. On the back of the furniture warehouse building facing 7<sup>th</sup> Ave are airbrushed portraits of those who have died with *Rest in Peace* tagged on the bottom in between angel wings that look like they are guiding the dead to heaven. In more graffiti lettering someone also added: *May the suits, the saints, and even the sinners bless the souls of those gone too soon.*

**21st Ave**

For some, dying on the Aves isn't much worse than living, and for others, life is short anyway, so rules are meant to be broken. At least that's how Lisa's house is run. It is a house with basically no rules and it is the most entertaining house on my block. Her parents often act like teenagers, fighting in the street, then making out in the street all during the same argument. Sometimes when the TV is broken and no amount of messing with the antennae can get it to work, I can just watch Lisa's family airing their dirty laundry and it is far more amusing than *The Love Boat*.

Eventually Lisa, tired of their curbside show, comes raging up the street yelling at them to stop. As if she's the parent and they're her kids, a mix of, "Why must you do this? Why do you have to act this way? Can't you just stop? Just stop!" can be heard echoing through the alley of the Aves. Sooner or later they will all fight their way back to the house, Lisa's mom crying, Lisa's dad yelling, Lisa yelling too, but no longer at them; from her front lawn, Lisa fires off at the neighbors who are unaffected and unwilling to move. Their windows are like televisions and Lisa is the leading lady.

"What are you looking at? Can't afford a TV? Never seen people fight? Nosey, just plain stinkin' nosey."

The thing is, Lisa can get away with talking to people like that, even adults. And sometimes her outburst is worse because her parents let her say the words that no kid gets to say, the ones with four or five letters, some ending in K or others beginning with B. Her mom even lets her say them in the house. She says they're just words and no one can decide what words can or can't be used. Because of this Lisa's place has become the cursing place. It is where we all go to practice new curse words learned from street corners and school and most of the time from Lisa. She explains how to use the words and where to stress certain letters for the ultimate effect. For Lisa it is all about the threat behind the word and the appearance that she can back up her words with action.

Physically Lisa is not very threatening at all. Barely taller than the roof of the family car and thin up and down with ankles the size of most people's wrists, to think of someone being scared of her is laughable. But even so, something in Lisa stirs up fear. There is an intensity inside her that explodes from her mouth and eyes and even her long spiraled hair that frizzes on the end like ropes set on fire. Something in Lisa makes us push only so far because there is something in Lisa that no one wants to see. Lisa pushes back. And to make up for when we teased her about her rhythmless dance, she practices and practices and practices some more, becoming one of the best dancers on the Aves, proving that the girl with the white mom and the Black dad has the beat running through her veins as constant and strong as the rest of us. It often takes little more than Lisa's sharp look or sharper tongue to wipe the smirks off our faces and keep us dancing with our mouths closed.

Lisa is not even scared of boys. Last week James's homeboy Q called Lisa a string bean and she attacked him in the middle of 3rd Avenue Park. Like a tractor or a lawnmower, the grumbling under her breath was the start of an engine and then she just plowed over the top of him so fast she had to reverse back to hit him head on. Kicking and scratching with Q screaming like a preschool girl, she pounded into him. Lisa was the hammer and Q the nail. Because he was bigger than her he finally managed to wrap his legs around hers and roll her beneath him. This was when the situation turned from bad to worse. You could see in his eyes that Q was thinking of all the things that had been told to him that he couldn't do to a girl and his thoughts quickly narrowed his options of revenge. This caused Q to let out a disappointed sigh as he sat on top of Lisa, pressing her wrists into the dirt with the palms of his hands. He finally gave up and pressed Lisa firmly into the ground as he pushed the weight of his body up into the air and off of her. Lisa quickly rolled into a seated position and tightened her ponytail that had loosened during the fight. She got to her feet, much slower this time, but it did not appear that she was hurt, more like possessed by a plan. She headed in the direction of Q, who had now turned his back and was walking toward the sand pit.

"Turn around, man! She's coming. Her crazy ass is coming for you."

Q spun around after the warnings from James and Aaron, but by then it was too late. Lisa was on the tips of her toes, nose to nose with Q.

"Just give it up, Lisa. I already pinned you. I already freakin' pinned you."

Lisa stood up on her toes even higher this time, as high as she could go, and then she leaned in as if going for a Hulk Hogan head butt and kissed him. Q's knees buckled beneath him, making him closer to Lisa's height, and what started out as a peck became a kiss you only see in movies or in the window of Tony and Roxanne's apartment. It was clear his tongue was inside her mouth and hers inside of his. With James and Aaron cheering them on Lisa had proven to the Aves once and for all she wasn't scared of anything, even boys.

**22nd Ave**

It is at Lisa's house in between bouts of curse word training that I tell her, Jeanine, and Janet about my conversation with the Peacock. My Imani secret also tears at my insides, but I need Mercy's help and even the spirit of Sauda to handle that dilemma.

"So you're just going to hang out with the crazy old lady?" says Janet.

"She's a freak!" exclaims Jeanine.

"You guys, she used to be an almost famous lounge singer. She has stories. Adult ones, and she isn't all weird about sharing them."

"I don't care what she used to be. She is nuts now," replies Lisa.

"Well it doesn't matter because she's gone back inside for the winter, but she gave me a job. She assigned me the task of writing down one experience each day and she says it will help me tap into my hidden gifts, something about branding my brilliance on paper."

The girls are no longer listening. The gossip of Lisa and Q's kiss is still the hottest topic. But for me, I am trying to find my inner Peacock. While she writes in the summer, on the porch, in her housecoat, puffing her up like a bag of Cheetos, my writing will happen during the school months, where she promised me a dollar a page. The only problem is by the end of my first week I have only recorded one line:

*September 10, 1987*

*Today I saw …*

It isn't that I didn't see anything, but the things I see don't seem important enough to write down. I imagine things written on paper should be more significant than grocery lists or homework assignments. At the end of each week I am supposed to stick my writing in between her screen and the door. The next day she will leave an envelope for me in the same spot. This week I only make 50 cents, but the envelope carries the heavy weight of failure.

Today in Mrs. Barnes's class we are assigned to read current events in the newspaper. By the time the newspaper gets around to me, the only section left is the obituaries.

Los Angeles – *Graveside services for Leo Brown, 82, will be at 1 p.m. on Friday at South Hill Park Memorial Cemetery in Los Angeles, CA. Born August 11, 1915, in Louisville, Kentucky, he moved to Los Angeles in 1966. He was a cook in the US Army.*

Los Angeles – *Elena Woods, 63, died Monday, September 5, 1987. Survivors include two daughters, one son, one brother, and three grandchildren. She was a homemaker.*

Now these are the things worth writing down. A life in four lines leaves no room for rambling. The most important things must rise to the surface, and when my story is told I want it to be told differently. Who cares when I was born? Who cares when I died? If my life can be summed up by my sunrise and my sunset, was it really a life worth living? I am sure Elena was a great homemaker, but she was surely much more than that. Maybe she was a Scrabble champion coming up with words that no one could match. Maybe she was in the Guinness Book of Records for the largest collection of California Raisin figures. When my few lines are written, in the *LA Times* or maybe in some other big-time newspaper, the world will be told:

The Aves – *A celebration of life is to be held for Zora Neale Rebecca Hunter. Zora was more than a homemaker, wife, and mother. She was a friend to all who knew her, a talented* *and famous Broadway choreographer, a Pac Man phenom and a voice for LA's Aves, now the most recognized neigh-borhood in Los Angeles. 10<sup>th</sup> Ave will be renamed Zora Blvd. in her honor. She is survived by five children, a husband, one sister, and countless friends.*

After I write my own obituary I write ones for others on the Aves.

The Aves – *Tony Sims died yesterday surrounded by the love of his life, his wife of 49 years, and his three sons. As a retired Marine, he personally presided over the community garden, where he nurtured his wife's favored white roses. He was a soldier but he was always a man of peace.*

The Aves – *Angela, pronounced Anhella, Viramontes has died at the age of 83. The modeling industry was devastated by the loss of one of the most distinctive fashion models of the 20<sup>th</sup> century. With the upcoming release of her newest line of hair care products Angela has many young girls look-ing to continue her legacy. Her siblings and a host of friends survive her.*

The Aves – *Isabelle Payne, also known as the Peacock, died today in her home, on 10<sup>th</sup> Ave, building 108. A writer of songs, she watched over the neighborhood with a pen and pad, turning the lives of those who lived around her into lyric and verse. She will be laid to rest in a private ceremony*

*but her stoop and her writing stool will forever represent
her scrolled tales of young dreamers searching for a better
way.*

This week I make a full four dollars.

**23rd Ave**

Imani's rescue doesn't go as planned, but probably because I have no plan. I wrestle with my thoughts of how to help Imani while also keeping her sacred secret. But for Mercy, there is no such sanctity in secrets. Things are truly black or white, wrong or right. In the absence of shades of gray, decision making is far more expeditious.

"What's wrong with you? Why are you pacing back and forth? You keep it up and you're going to mess up the lines in my carpet!"

"It's just …"

"Spit it out, Zora."

"It's about Imani."

And that's about all I remember. The words just stormed out my mouth as if on a starting block: on your marks, get set, go! And just as frantic as my spilled beans, Mercy marches over to Imani's house, grabs all of Imani's stuff, escorts Imani back to our house, charges back into

Imani's house, smashes a bottle of Jack Daniels sitting on the front ledge, and she does this all in the time it would take to run a 400-meter relay. As predicted, her dad's liver continues to fail but Mercy says his heart failed first. We officially become Imani's Avenue family, and I finally understand the preoccupation Prose has with me as a big sister. Big sisters lead the way with long legs that make shadows for little sisters to play in.

I now exist in the land of the in between. A big sister and a little sister who isn't 10 anymore with braided wings. Instead I'm 13 and I've grown into the ritual of hair wrapping, sleeping bonnets, and twice-monthly trips to the salon. When I go now, I look forward to the gossip exchanged between grown folks talkin' about grown folks' business. Taking mental notes, peacocking and waiting in between washes. In the waiting is where I learn that I like the texture of my pre-pressed hair too. It's thicker, mightier; it soaks up the strawberry suds the way I dreamt it could do. And it doesn't blow away the moment the breeze rushes in. It goes out and comes back like hundreds of powerful boomerangs. This is what I should tell Prose on the eve of her 10th birthday as Imani and I sit unbraiding her pigtails. But unlike me at that age, Prose isn't afraid at all. Her nonchalance makes me forewarn of a more ominous order of events.

I remind her that she has to listen when Ms. Felicia says, "Don't move."

"Even if you feel like you aren't moving, still don't move!"

She laughs and her chuckles mix in with Imani's. I continue my lecture, pretending to be a teacher at the head of the class.

"Okay, listen up, students. Today my lesson plan will focus on beauty shop procedures. Pay close attention because there might be a quiz at the end.

"Step one: There is this oven, but not like a turkey-basting, cookie-baking, full-size oven you see in a kitchen. This oven is the size of a shoe and has a tiny oval-shaped mouth with metal legs that sit on the counter. The mouth of the oven stays open as if it's eating up the heat and hair and metal combs made for pressing."

At this point Prose stops smiling.

"Step two: By this time your hair will be washed, which is the fun part because Ms. Felicia's daughter lathers up a bunch of bubbles, like when Mercy puts dishwashing liquid in the tub. She makes your hair soapy-white all while singing 'Cool It Now' and other songs by New Edition. She says she is going to marry Ralph Tresvant. I don't even think she knows him, but she's a good singer anyway. When she is done washing your hair, she puts a plastic cap over your head and sits you under a big hair dryer. It's hot but sometimes on a cold day it actually feels like a heater warming you from your head all the way down to your toes."

With focused and less laughing eyes, Prose asks, "Will Ms. Felicia's daughter sing to me too?"

"Trust me, she'll sing whether you want her to or not. There will be singing and cursing and stories that start and stop and start again interspersed with, 'Hey, turn that radio up! That's my song!'

"Step three: After you are dry you'll sit in Ms. Felicia's chair, which spins around, but don't you ever spin it yourself. Let her do everything to you and sit real still so you don't get burned. Do you understand? The key objective the entire time you are there is to not get burned. Then, she will part your hair into different sections and begin to press the parts from your scalp down to your ends. It's kind of like when Mercy or I comb your hair, but this time the comb will be fiery hot.

"So, that's pretty much it." I cut my step-by-step guide short because the amusement has lifted and is replaced with a hint of hypothetical doom.

"Man, Zora. You didn't have to school her like that."

"It's all good. You're good, right, Prose?"

My assurance is met with a pensive Prose running her fingers through her loose hair.

25th Ave

The following day, Prose is nowhere to be found. I convince Mercy to throw her a party for being such a big girl, but Prose, who would never dare miss a celebration in her honor, is gone. I look for her in every hiding place she likes to use. The closets, beneath her bed, under the dining table. I peek out the front door like Mercy's distrust of weather reports taught us to do. Prose isn't on the porch checking for precipitation. On my way back in, Mercy is storming out. The look on her face – eyes squinting with her nostrils flared as if she is trying to breathe through her nose – makes her appear crazed. A lifetime of anxieties erupts into lava.

"Something is wrong. It's not right. It's wrong. I can feel it. Stay right here," she says.

"But –"

"Zora Neale, I'm your mother. I just told you to do something. Take your behind to that couch and sit there."

Something is wrong. The way Mercy called herself my "mother" shifted the ground beneath me.

I haven't seen Mercy run since I was very little. I remember she used to chase us around the house pretending to be a starved tickle monster whose appetite could only be fed by the giggles of squealing girls. But lately no more running or hungry creatures, just a fast, hip-swinging walk when she's late for work. Looking out the window, I see her run like a baseball player heading into home plate. Her backside looks like it is inches behind the rest of her body and her neck curves all the way around the block before she does.

And then she screams.

Mercy's scream ricochets in reverse back into our living room. I follow her scream like a song on repeat until I see the flashing lights and familiar yellow tape zigzagging toward me. When I get closer, I see Mercy on her knees pounding her fist into the concrete. There is broken glass and twisted metal everywhere. The crowd of people standing around look more like shapes than humans. What was once in color has now become shades of black, gray, and white. Everything has lost its form.

Tony is there. Like a guard he stands in front of me. We dance. If I go right, the shoulder of his uniform goes left, then his right, then my left. Eventually he loses the rhythm and I slide by him as he pleads, "Zora, wait. Please wait."

Tony's tears are a part of a flood that sweeps through all the Aves. I swim into the blackness but not before seeing a tiny body covered by a white sheet. I know Prose is under there, but she looks so much smaller than someone turning 10.

In her pants pocket the officers find a sandwich bag filled with barrettes labeled for Babygirl. Prose wanted to give Babygirl the hair clips that she no longer needed. I'll never know why she didn't wait for me or why she felt she was somehow old enough to cross this street. But one thing is clear: death is sneaky, and it doesn't play fair. And now the bricks I carry, from a lifetime on the Aves, crumble into smashed clay.

**26th Ave**

The week leading up to the funeral is a full house of constant heads that pop up behind pots and plants and so many flowers that the smells are in competition with one another. People come from far outside the Aves to hug me and touch my face and feed me and then rub my face as if to make sure that I too don't fade away. Mercy won't get out of bed, lying on her back with her eyes wide open; she is stiller than the dead and she is cold. To get away from the face-touching do-gooders, I vacuum. I try to keep the carpet lines the way Mercy likes, but the footprints keep coming. I never know the time or what day of the week it is. One morning I just see Mercy out of bed and ironing my black funeral dress.

The Star Cruiser is already inside the church when we get there. He takes off his hat, a black fedora, and places it over his heart. He almost looks like he is preparing to pledge allegiance when Mercy collapses into his arms.

The feather on his hat crumples from the weight of their embrace. This is the first time I have ever seen my parents hug. My eyes are fixed on the feather, copper like Prose's penny-colored eyes. After what seems like forever, for me and the feather, they let go. Imani ushers in the guests by playing Sauda's guitar.

Prose's death brings out everyone. The sick. The shut-in. Imani's father, in a wheelchair now but clean shaven and sober; the Peacock, Lou, the 2nd Ave crew, and Jeanine and Janet with a bouquet stuffed in an empty bottle of Fanta from ToGo. There are too many people and the church has to place extra chairs out on the sidewalk and church lawn when the sanctuary begins to overflow with mourners. During Pastor Baldwin's eulogy I can feel the heaviness of my eyelids. I am too exhausted to cry. I want to sleep. Smashed between the shoulders of Mercy and the Star Cruiser I drift into a dream where Prose and I are window-walking. We are all grown, but Prose's face still looks 10 and we are cracking up at a woman throwing her husband's shoes out the window. The man comes running down the stairs frantically scooping up his Nikes, but when he passes us he walks through Prose as if she isn't even there.

When I open my eyes, the small casket is covered in a sunburst of colors from the stained glass windows. Prose is high in the sanctuary, cradled in a bed of light. Like life, she handles death with a brilliant brightness, flying away on a rainbow with no beginning and no end. By the time

James, Uncle Ricky, the Star Cruiser, and the other pall-bearers carry her casket down the aisle her soul is already free.

The doors of the church open up into the biggest celebration the Aves has ever seen. Balloons and streamers into the hundreds sway in the breeze. Lisa is dancing and she signals Jeanine, Janet, and me into the beat. At a distance a little girl spins round and round. She is like a sprinkler on a hot Los Angeles day spraying the streets with her cascade of braids. At least a dozen car speakers blast a Stephanie Mills song that Mercy adored: "I Never Knew Love Like This Before." Mustering a miraculous joy that felt as supercharged as the electric slide, Mercy winks at me and then she cries, "For Prose, now we party!"

# Acknowledgments

Like intersections of city streets, this novella would not have been possible without the convergence of the following supporters:

To Leapfrog Press, thank you for such a rewarding publishing experience. To Tobias, Nicole, Sarah, and the entire team, you have filled this process with immeasurable care and enthusiasm.

To Brenda Patterson, judge of the 2023 Leapfrog Press Global Fiction Prize, thank you for your insightful feedback and for believing in my story.

To Kareem Tayyar, thank you for your unwavering declaration that this book deserved to be out in the world. Your certainty in my characters gave me the confidence to start again.

To my artistic allies in Women Who Submit, thank you for standing in solidarity with my words, cheering on every submission, and inspiring me with your collective talents.

# Acknowledgments

To Oksana Marafioti, thank you for using your editorial eye to help my words travel in time.

To my mentors and fellow writers who convinced me this story needed to be written and encouraged my efforts along the way: Alma Luz Villanueva, Ruth Forman, Tisha Marie Reichle-Aguilera, Xochitl-Julisa Bermejo, Noriko Nakada, bridgette bianca, Keisha Cosand, Lucy Rodriguez-Hanley, Aruni Wijesinghe, and Xoaquima Diaz, I can't say thank you enough.

To my former writing group members who were generous with their feedback, their writing spaces, and their snacks: Cassandra Lane Rich, Jennifer Genest, Ramona Wright, and LaCoya Katoe Gessesse, thank you for your critiques.

To the outlets who've provided opportunities for me to share excerpts of this story: Cody Sisco, David Rocklin, and Mensah Demary, thank you for amplifying my words.

To Mommy, thank you for teaching me how to dream with my eyes open. Thank you also for running ahead at times, clearing a path as I chased my dreams.

To Grammy, thank you for calling me "writer." You planted the seeds long ago. Can you see the harvest in heaven? I hope so.

To my children, thank you for sharpening my perspective, deepening my laugh lines, and being the best plot twists of my life.

To my husband, Joe, thank you for loving this LA girl, and for building shelves for my books and a refuge for my dreams.

# About the author

Ryane Nicole Granados has always called Los Angeles her home and her writing finds its roots in her love of community. She is inspired to write stories of survival that magnify the marginalized while also unearthing the splendor of second chances.

Ryane earned her MFA in Creative Writing from Antioch University, Los Angeles, and she was named the 2021 Established Writer and Individual Arts Fellow by the California Arts Council. Currently, Ryane teaches at Loyola Marymount University, where she also serves as the associate director of the Academic Resource Center and Writing Center. Her literary work has been featured in various publications including *Pangyrus*, *The Manifest-Station*, *High Country News*, *The Atticus Review*, and *LA Parent Magazine*. Her storytelling has also been nominated for a Pushcart Prize and showcased in KPCC's live series Unheard LA.

## About the author

In addition to her longstanding commitment to writing and teaching, Ryane has served as the Chapters Director for the literary non-profit Women Who Submit (WWS): an organization empowering women and non-binary writers to submit their work for publication. Recently she also served as the co-managing editor for the third WWS anthology, *Transformation*. Previous WWS anthologies have been featured on the Community of Literary Magazines and Presses Year End List of Hybrid Works, Anthologies & Children's Books.

When not writing or teaching, Ryane can be found transporting her children to school, sports fields, band practices, or playdates. As a mother of five, she views preserving the aspirations of all children as an act of social justice.

Printed in the USA
CPSIA information can be obtained
at www.ICGtesting.com
JSHW021911070924
69463JS00001B/1